TREASURE HUNTERS

The Truth

E. A. HOUSE

EPIC Escape

An Imprint of EPIC Press
abdopublishing.com

The Truth

Treasure Hunters: Book #5

Written by E. A. House

Copyright © 2018 by Abdo Consulting Group, Inc.

Published by EPIC Press™
PO Box 398166
Minneapolis, MN 55439

Cover design by Laura Mitchell
Images for cover art obtained from iStock and Shutterstock
Edited by Ryan Hume

LIBRARY OF CONGRESS CATALOGING-IN-PUBLICATION DATA
Names: House, E.A., author.
Title: The truth/ by E.A. House
Description: Minneapolis, MN : EPIC Press, 2018 | Series: Treasure hunters; #5
Summary: Chris and Carrie have been betrayed. Maddison has discovered the dark secret in
   her father's past. As a crime wave hits Archer's Grove and authorities struggle to catch the
   culprits, Chris, Carrie, and Maddison turn to the Kingsolvers' Aunt Elsie for answers.
Identifiers: LCCN 2017949811 | ISBN 9781680768800 (lib. bdg.)
   | ISBN 9781680768947 (ebook)
Subjects: LCSH: Adventure stories—Fiction. | Code and cipher stories—Fiction.
   | Family secrets—Fiction. | Treasure troves—Fiction | Young adult fiction.
Classification: DDC [FIC]—dc23
LC record available at http://lccn.loc.gov/2017949811

For librarians everywhere

CHAPTER ONE

"You would think that with the police, the FBI, and the Coast Guard all in the same building nobody would be able to quietly step out a side door and disappear," Chris Kingsolver said.

For once he wasn't talking about Dr. McRae, who was sitting stoically on Detective Hermann's desk and had been since before Chris and Carrie had arrived at the station. In the interest of not having everyone's stories get mixed up, Agent Grey had very firmly placed the Kingsolvers at one desk and the McRaes at another and ordered them not to talk to one another. So, Chris wasn't *absolutely* certain that

Dr. McRae wasn't doing anything suspicious. But he really meant Robin Redd. Somewhere between the Coast Guard meeting the *Meandering Manatee* at the mouth of the harbor and Chris and Carrie being escorted into the police station by a federal agent who had her hand glued to the gun on her hip, Robin Redd had managed to disappear.

"It's not disappearing, exactly," Bethy sighed. "I think, at least. He said, 'Oh my goodness the Grey Cove shots,' and made a beeline for the rental car place, and to be honest, he really has to be at Grey Cove or we won't be able to shoot there, and I'm not sure we'd get anything coherent out of him anyway, so . . . "

Detective Hermann looked like he wanted to argue, but had met Redd before, and so couldn't really. "If we could just get a clear story out of each of you, that would be very helpful," he said instead, looking from Carrie to Chris to Bethy.

Chris and Carrie shared a worried look. They had both spent several weeks trying to keep different things secret from different people; had told several different variations of what was essentially a lie, and if not quite a lie, a very misleading statement; and were now not entirely sure what they had told to whom, and when. Chris felt very much like that time he had tripped over a rubber bouncy ball while carrying a fully loaded tray of tea cups—in the split second just before all of the cups hit the floor and shattered, when he saw what was about to happen but couldn't do anything to stop it.

"Well," he said.

"You see," Carrie started.

"I have absolutely no idea what's going on," Bethy admitted. One desk over, Dr. McRae looked like he would rather be anywhere but there, and Maddison looked as though she'd had a minor revelation. Detective Hermann looked from one desk to the other, and sighed.

"Well, this is going to be a *loooong* night," he said.

In the end, Chris and Carrie told the detective the truth, but without bringing the *San Telmo* into the story. Most people didn't immediately assume the two scared and still-damp kids had been looking for a lost treasure ship, and it was pretty easy to skate around *why* the professor had decided to leave them in the ocean. So, Chris and Carrie told Detective Hermann that they'd been accompanying the professor and some grad students who were supposed to be studying coastal erosion, and that the professor had gotten a fake grad student to throw them overboard. They did *not* say that they suspected it was so that they couldn't interfere with the professor's hunt for the *San Telmo*. As for the other pieces of the story, they had nothing to hide. They'd met Bethy and the currently AWOL Redd on a camping trip recently, they'd fallen down the well in the cistern at Saint Erasmus while doing research for a school project, and they'd been threatened, recently, by the same man who had killed their aunt.

"Uh-huh," Detective Hermann said.

"We did do a little research into the *San Telmo* when we were doing that school project," Chris offered, hoping desperately that the detective wasn't about to see through him and demand that he stop looking for the *San Telmo* altogether. "But I don't know *why* Professor Griffin is so obsessed with it."

"Willis Griffin is a very obsessed individual," Agent Grey said, startling everyone. She'd folded herself into a chair next to Detective Hermann just as he was starting to question Chris and Carrie. One desk over, her partner appeared to be doing the same thing with Maddison and her family. But the instant Agent Grey had sat down she'd faded into the background almost completely. It was a terrifying skill to have, and Chris could see why it would be useful for a law enforcement official.

"Griffin's dangerous. He's intelligent, he's driven, and for some reason he's convinced that you two are the key to his delusions," Agent Grey went on. "And as of this moment he's in the wind. Harvey Tanner called the first Kingsolver phone number he found." She gave Carrie a look, and Carrie clapped both hands over her mouth in horror as she realized what she meant—that Harvey Tanner had called *her* parents. "But aside from a sobbing confession and repeated insistence that he didn't mean to do it, we haven't been able to get anything else out of him. Figuring out where he parted with Griffin and where Griffin is now will take us a while, and in the meantime you should probably have a police escort."

"Agent Grey means all of you," Detective Hermann said, raising his voice so that Agent Holland stopped talking quietly with Dr. McRae, and turned towards Detective Hermann.

"Yes, especially the people who have unpleasant history with Griffin," Agent Grey agreed, giving Dr. McRae a significant look.

"I can't force you to accept," Detective Hermann added. "Especially not when we have no real proof you're going to be in danger, but I don't like the way you've been targeted."

Dr. McRae looked uncertainly at his wife.

"I especially don't like the way you seem to attract trouble," the detective added, and actually smiled at the way Maddison's mom stomped on her husband's foot when he did.

"Ow—I assure you, Detective," Dr. McRae said, hopping a little on one foot, "no member of the McRae family will be doing any funny business, especially since you've got an equally good reason to put cars outside the Kingsolver residences. That'll cut down on Maddison's reason for wandering."

Oh no, Chris thought. *Parents.* Everything had happened so fast that he hadn't had a chance to worry about how his parents were going to react to Chris and his cousin falling overboard, or the fact that it was Professor Griffin's fault.

Chris got Detective Hermann as his police escort. Detective Hermann also brought along an Officer Carson, who was going to be watching the house—if the Kingsolvers agreed to it—but Chris got the police detective instead of the FBI agents because Harvey had not called *his* parents in a panic and confessed to throwing Chris and Carrie overboard. Which wasn't even what had happened! Nobody had *thrown* Chris overboard at all; he'd jumped in himself . . . which was maybe not a useful clarification. Agents Grey and Holland had volunteered to take Carrie home because "we've handled these kinds of scenes before," according to Agent Grey.

So, all things considered, it was a little insulting when the first word out of his mom's mouth when she opened the door to find Chris on the doorstep with a police escort was, "Oh Lord, what did he *do*?"

Significantly more alarming was the fact that Officer Carson replied with complete honesty, "Almost drowned, ma'am," because then his mom actually did—not panic, exactly, she could see that Chris was all right so she wasn't about to go into hysterics—but she did drag Chris into a hug. Detective Hermann rubbed his temples and grimaced.

"What was Willis doing while this was going on?" Chris's mom demanded, looking Detective Hermann in the eye and proving that things were actually capable of getting even more awkward. Chris bit his lip. There was no *good* way to fill his mom in. *So, remember how Aunt Elsie died last month? Well about that . . .*

No. Just, simply, no. Even Chris knew that that was a terrible idea.

"Willis Griffin is currently under investigation," Detective Hermann said firmly. "He has also gone missing, so for the foreseeable future, Officer Carson here is going to be watching your house."

"Oh-kay," Chris's mom said. "And is he watching the house to keep us safe from whatever happened to Willis, or to keep us safe *from* Willis?"

Detective Hermann sighed.

"Professor Griffin got a fake grad student to push Carrie off the boat," Chris said to his toes. Ringing silence followed his pronouncement, and Chris finally looked up to discover that Detective

Hermann was making notes in his notebook and smiling slightly and his mom was turning an interesting shade of red.

"He. Did. *What?*" Then she made an aborted attempt to grab an umbrella from the stand and march out into the night to track Professor Griffin down herself, having apparently decided to get right to the heart of the problem and not even bother about the fake grad student. Chris grabbed her sweatshirt sleeve and Officer Carson stepped awkwardly and uncomfortably in front of the door. Chris's mom sagged and lowered the umbrella.

"It's not like I was going to do anything permanent to him," she said.

Officer Carson did not look convinced. But Chris's mom put the umbrella back in the umbrella stand and stopped looking like she was going to charge out of the house in bare feet and very bright pink pajama pants and a "National Square-Dancing Championships 2009" T-shirt, so he stepped away from the door, relieved.

"Carrie's fine!" Chris offered. "We both are. Redd . . . there was another boat in the area and they picked us up before anything could happen. We just got wet." Better not mention Robin Redd just yet.

"What were you *both* doing in the water?"

"Hey, where's Dad?" Chris asked desperately, as Detective Hermann bit back a laugh. Chris never exactly forgot that his mom was driven. After all, she was the driving force behind the Kingsolvers winning ribbons in the national square-dancing competition three years in a row. But he'd been so busy with the mystery of the *San Telmo* that he'd slipped up and forgotten how very good she was at catching when you were trying to hide a secret from her by not mentioning it at all.

"He put earplugs in because I was watching a movie and he wanted to sleep," Chris's mom explained absently, which meant that Chris's dad was going to sleep through his alarm and be very confused later this morning, so it was a good thing it was a Saturday night. "Did Willis push you in, as well? Or did you jump over the side?"

"I jumped," Chris admitted.

"Hm."

"I know, I should have stayed on the ship and thrown a life preserver."

"No," his mom said thoughtfully. "Going overboard was probably the best option." Then she made sensible arrangements with Detective Hermann, gave Officer Carson a cup of tea, and shooed everyone off while Chris was still wondering what her thought processes were.

"Oh, and Chris?" his mom added on her way back to bed for half an hour more of sleep. "The bakery sent you a letter with interview times, so you need to get on that this week."

✗ ✗ ✗

He did not tell his mom about Robin Redd, and it wasn't for any specific reason. Chris simply wasn't sure what to make of Robin Redd, also known as Robin Wyzowski, also known as the host of the world's worst exploration documentary-drama currently on television. Redd seemed to be a genuinely decent, if overly dramatic, sort of person, and Chris hadn't forgotten that the television star had tackled a gun-wielding maniac for him.

But then Redd had disappeared on the way to the police station. With the most natural alibi in the world, true, but if—as Chris suspected—Robin Redd was actually much smarter than his random wandering and overly dramatic announcements made him seem, then he must have had a reason for disappearing like that. And Chris was getting to the point where he didn't trust anyone's reasons until he could see them for himself. It was also more than a little odd that Robin Redd had happened to be out on the ocean at the exact moment Chris and Carrie desperately needed to be rescued—and what self-respecting B-rate television star would shy away from publicity, especially publicity of the completely complimentary type resulting from the heroic rescue of two teenagers from the sea?

Something just didn't add up, and Chris was not going to drag Robin Redd into it until he figured it out. Also, his father hated Robin Redd and his television show with an undying passion, and Chris and Carrie still hadn't told their parents about meeting Robin Redd and his entire film crew in the woods. Or about how the producer Harry Bradlaw had almost shot Chris. So mentioning Robin Redd by name, Chris told himself, would mean that he'd have to explain why he knew Robin Redd, and how they met, and then that would lead to uncomfortable questions about why he hadn't told anyone about nearly getting shot, and then Chris's mom would probably decide to go after Professor Griffin, the fake grad students, *and* Harry Bradlaw, as well. Chris liked Bethy Bradlaw far too much to set his mother on her brother, even accidentally.

But still. What was Robin Redd so worried about?

CHAPTER TWO

CARRIE CLIMBED IN CHRIS'S WINDOW AT TEN THE next morning. This was alarming for two reasons: first, because Chris had only fallen asleep at four in the morning the previous night, and second, because Carrie was followed closely by Maddison, and Chris was still in his pajamas.

"Um, hi?" Chris said as Maddison dragged herself through his window, landed on his feet, and rolled off his bed and face-first onto the floor, where she dug her fingers into the fibers of his rug and grumbled.

"It's much harder to sneak out of your house

when there is a very nice police officer waiting out- side to make sure Professor Griffin doesn't try his hand at arson," Carrie said instead of saying anything sensible, like "Good morning."

"Please make more sense," Chris said. "It's too early for this."

"*Sleeeeeep*," Maddison mumbled, either in agree- ment with Chris or just because she hadn't had very much. Her face wasn't visible and Chris's vision was still blurry with sleep. Then she dragged herself into a sitting position against the desk, and blinked at Carrie. "And why were you avoiding the police? I told the officer where I was going and she radioed the one sitting across the street from your house."

Carrie pointed directly at Chris. "Sorry, force of habit," she said.

"*Why* are you guys *here*?" Chris asked. They really did have a habit of doing this to him; he felt like he was missing out on a group text or something. And he was missing out on precious sleep, and probably going to get a cold from ending up in the water last night with no warning.

"We have only a very limited window of time before the police and the FBI start locking down the crime scenes," Maddison said, as Carrie scooted under Chris's desk and pried up the floorboard that he hid most of their *San Telmo* research under. "So, if we want to get any further with the *San Telmo*, then we need to do it today. Especially since the police and the FBI know about the *San Telmo* now," she said, and then she winced at Chris's alarmed face. "Which I refuse to feel guilty about," she added, "because getting it out of my dad was like pulling teeth and there was a lot of crying and—and—" She was starting to hyperventilate.

"Breathe," Carrie said. "It's okay, nobody *actually* got eaten by a shark, we're all fine, just take deep breaths."

"Sorry."

"It's really not a problem," Chris said as gently as he could. He wasn't the best at it; he'd been told he switched between goofy and stubborn and not much else. Maddison gave him a slightly shaky smile anyway.

"I kept calling you and calling you and nobody ever picked up—your parents must all think I'm nuts—and then we got back to Florida and you were *missing at sea*!" Maddison threw her hands in the air. "It's only a *little* Victorian-sounding!"

"Meh," Carrie said. "We've lost at least six ancestors that way."

"Five," Chris said. "Athanasius Kingsolver faked his death, I keep telling you this—"

"Athanasius Kingsolver was trying to smuggle turtles across the Atlantic, *why* would you tell everyone you were going to make your fortune on turtles and then fake your own death?"

"Because he finally realized that smuggling snapping turtles was not a viable business plan?" Chris suggested. Carrie growled at him.

"My great-great-great grandmother rode a horse backwards through her little village, covered in ivy, to break a family curse," Maddison said. "But we were talking about the *San Telmo*, not the, err . . ."

"His ship was called the *Tortuga*," Chris supplied helpfully.

Maddison gave him a narrow-eyed look. "It was, was it?"

"*Anyway*," Carrie said before Chris could drag another person into his ongoing conspiracy theory about Athanasius Kingsolver. "Despite the forty-five minutes Chris spent last week reading Wikipedia articles about Cesar Francisco, it's pretty obviously not him that they found in the church cistern, which suggests it's one of the missing persons from the nineties." She shook the pile of missing-persons posters out of the folder they'd been in and across the floor. "Which suggests that it's actually . . . "

"Ryan Moore," Maddison said, picking up the poster with his face smiling up at them and running a finger over his name at the bottom.

Carrie blinked at her—why did Maddison seem so sure? "He went missing in the early nineties."

"He went missing in the early nineties," Maddison agreed. "They only just got the dental scans back and confirmed that it was him, I . . . " She blushed slightly. "I overheard one of the police officers complaining about the fax machine and the information just slipped out." She handed Carrie the missing-persons poster. "Ryan Moore was a friend of my dad's, and Professor Griffin's, and he must have stumbled across something that got him killed."

"Maddison," Chris asked, "what did your dad tell you about what happened between him and Professor Griffin?"

"They were friends in college," Maddison said. "My dad told me what he knows about what happened to Ryan Moore, but it's not much. He hasn't got a clue where the treasure of the *San Telmo* is, and he doesn't even know why everyone thought he"— she bit her lip—"thought he killed Ryan Moore."

When the person who really did was right in front of us the whole time, Chris thought. It wasn't much of a leap to assume that Professor Griffin killed Ryan

Moore, although that did lead directly to the question of *why* the professor would want to kill him.

Chris pointed this out. Carrie suggested that he might be a little obsessed with the *San Telmo*. Chris replied that being obsessed with a sunken treasure ship didn't necessarily mean that you wanted to kill a friend.

"Maybe he killed Ryan Moore because Ryan was interested in the *San Telmo* too?" Maddison suggested. "That's about all I know about him—that he was a friend of my dad's, and that he was almost as into treasure hunting as Professor Griffin was."

"Was *everybody* looking for the *San Telmo*?" Carrie wondered. "I mean, we have your dad, my aunt, Professor Griffin, this Ryan Moore person . . . "

"According to my dad, they were in a treasure-hunting club together," Maddison said.

"Wait, what?" Carrie said.

Chris opened his mouth to talk, but all he managed was a startled squeak.

"Um, I may have forgotten to mention that," Maddison muttered, turning red. "See, I finally got Dad to tell me how he knew your aunt."

"Oh jeez," Carrie said faintly.

"And next thing I know he's getting really upset over a bunch of people I only just recently met!" Maddison explained. "Apparently they were all in a class together, my dad, your aunt, Professor Griffin, someone else whose name I forget—it was Reminoski? Wolaski?—and Ryan Moore."

There was something tugging very faintly at Chris's mind. Why did Wolaski pluck at his thoughts so strangely? But then Maddison was talking again and he lost the thread.

"I just don't understand why the professor would kill him and then spend the next eighteen years waiting and doing nothing before he went looking for the *San Telmo*," Maddison added. "And I especially don't understand how he figured out what was going on. Your aunt hadn't been looking for the treasure."

"But she stumbled across it," Chris offered. "She

found the *San Telmo* when she was doing research for an exhibit . . . that the college was *behind*!"

"Huh?" Carrie asked. Chris threw his blankets off (they landed on Carrie) and yanked his computer out of the desk drawer.

"I didn't even remember it until just now," he said, "but I must have spent hours staring at this circling banner when I was thinking about Aunt Elsie's murder way back before all this treasure hunting started—and look at the donors!" He shoved the computer at Maddison, who squinted at the screen.

"The Edgewater Archive would like to thank Dr. Poteskin, the Atlantic Arts Museum, Archer's Grove Bar and Grill, and the Florida State Community Involvement Board for their support in the making of this exhibit," Maddison read. "Professor Griffin was . . ."

"Part of the Florida State Community Involvement Board," Carrie said, reading over her shoulder. "I can't believe we didn't catch this the first time!"

"Yes," Maddison said stubbornly, "but why did the professor decide to start killing people for the treasure? And did your aunt know? And more importantly, why did her notes lead to a parish register that ultimately led us nowhere?"

"And where did the professor go after he left us to drown in the ocean?" Chris said. Harvey had been apprehended, it was true, after he had called Carrie's parents in tears and confessed to being part of a plot to throw her overboard. So at least one of the professor's accomplices had gotten cold feet and broken with the others. But the professor was still at large, as was the ship, and Brad, the not-actually-a-grad-student.

"Um, I might have an answer to that," Carrie said. "But you aren't going to like it." Carrie pretty clearly didn't like it; she now looked miserable.

"Where Professor Griffin went?" Chris asked. "How would you—"

"I might have, um, sent the professor on a wild goose chase."

Chris and Maddison stared at her.

"I mean it's *possible* that I sent the professor on a wild goose chase," Carrie said miserably. "I *gave* him the coordinates to the *San Telmo*. If he hasn't found the ship yet then either there's nothing to find or I misunderstood the clues Aunt Elsie left, and the coordinates I came up with don't mean anything!"

"We'll figure it out," Chris said quickly, before Carrie could work herself into a panic attack over failing to get the coordinates right. If she actually had. Chris might sometimes consider his cousin a goody two-shoes but he did respect her intelligence, so if she couldn't find the *San Telmo* based on the information from the parish register and a lot of cross-referencing of mollusk breeding grounds then he didn't know who could. Maybe Professor Griffin had just read Carrie's notes wrong?

The suggestion didn't go over terribly well, but Carrie picked up on what he was trying to do and gave him a little half smile, so it was worth it.

"Anyway," she said, pulling herself together,

"we do need to decide what we're going to do next, because I for one would like to know what really happened with Ryan Moore and why Aunt Elsie never told anyone about it before we go looking for the ship again," she said. "Though, I don't want to go back on the water right away, not after what just happened."

"And I don't want to go anywhere without known cell reception until they catch the professor," Chris added. He did not say anything about getting back on the horse after it kicks you off, because he was not stupid. And neither was Carrie—if they needed to get on a boat, then she would handle it just fine. Until then it was just fine with Chris if they stayed on solid ground. He had miraculously avoided seasickness through medication and sheer confusion last time, and was not likely to be that lucky a second time. Much better that they stay on dry land and deal with the mystery here, even if it was a decades-old murder with a missing suspect.

The question, then, was what to do about the

decades-old murder with a missing suspect that was quickly going to become an active police investigation.

"The thing is, I'm not sure they're going to actually get Professor Griffin for everything he did," Maddison said. "I mean, there is no proof of a motive and he was never even a suspect last time . . . "

"Not if we have anything to say about it," Chris said reflexively, and then stopped. "Err. I mean . . . "

"*Aaaaargh*," Carrie said, pulling Chris's blankets off his bed and over her head. "I'm out of ideas. Leave me to die."

Maddison patted the blanket-covered lump gently on the head. "It might help if we could come up with a little more proof that the professor was mixed up in this whole thing from the beginning," she offered. "My dad apparently never told anyone about the *San Telmo* or the treasure hunting when Ryan disappeared."

"Do we *have* any more proof that the professor

was mixed up in this from the beginning?" Carrie asked. She had one eye peeking out from under the blankets and seemed to be slipping under the bed.

"We don't—but Aunt Elsie might," Chris said slowly. "I didn't throw out any of her papers, and I didn't even look at most of them! We should see if there's anything in her paperwork that could incriminate him."

× × ×

When Chris had packed up all of his aunt's things at the Archive, that time he had first met Dr. McRae, he had been far too upset and distracted to pay a lot of attention to where they went. He did register that his mom was planning to store most of the boxes at Aunt Elsie's house until the rest of the family was ready to face going through them, but she could have donated all the boxes to a monastery in Germany and Chris wouldn't have noticed. Still, it wasn't hard to guess that if Chris, Carrie, and Maddison wanted to find out if Aunt Elsie had left any suspicions of Professor Griffin's involvement behind they would need to search the six or seven cardboard boxes of her work supplies that had been left in the living room of her house, according to Chris's somewhat puzzled mom.

"I dropped them off when I had a free moment after work," she explained when Chris finally went in search of breakfast and took Carrie and Maddison with him. She was in the kitchen having toast, and she did a double-take at the sight of Carrie and Maddison. "Why didn't I hear you girls come in the door?"

Carrie froze in the middle of pouring herself a bowl of cereal, and Maddison just put her head in her hands.

"Anyway, we were hoping it'd be okay if we went and looked through some of that stuff from her office," Chris said in a rush, before his mom could demand to know how Carrie and Maddison had gotten in the house that morning.

"I'm doing some grocery shopping today," Chris's mom said, sliding a second bowl under Carrie's cereal box as the first started to overflow—Carrie was too horrified at the idea of her favorite entrance to the house being discovered to do so herself. "So, I can leave you three there for an hour and a half this afternoon, provided Officer Carson doesn't veto the idea." The second cereal bowl now filled, she gently tugged the cereal box out of Carrie's hand and set it on the counter. Then Chris's mom took the extra serving of Froot Loops and plunked it in front of Maddison.

"We'll pick you up on the way over if you want," she told Maddison as she handed her a spoon to go with the Froot Loops. "I'm heading out sometime between one and two o'clock. I'll make Chris text you when we're leaving."

After making a sizable dent in Chris's supply of Froot Loops, Carrie and Maddison both left. Carrie went to get a few hours of sleep and Maddison wanted to "reassure my dad that there were no

Professor Griffins hiding in the bushes." In the middle of their departure, Chris's dad had come dashing downstairs in a panic because he had the days confused and thought he was about to be late for work, getting almost out the door before Chris and his mom were able to stop him. His mom actually did need to finish some paperwork for work and so locked herself in her office. And then Chris had the house more or less to himself. He lasted about half an hour in the silence before he realized that he needed to do *something* or he was going to go nuts.

So he took a very hot shower in the forlorn hope of waking himself up a little, and then went in search of asters.

✗ ✗ ✗

There was another flower crown on Aunt Elsie's grave. It was fresh, too—the clovers and asters braided together still had sticky stems where they had been broken and none of the petals had yet begun to wilt in the Florida sun. Chris brushed dried-grass clippings off the grass in front of the grave and then carefully separated his own bouquet of asters into its individual flowers.

"Who keeps bringing you flower crowns?" Chris asked, scattering purple flowers across the grave. He was almost tempted to pluck and scatter the purple petals, but then he would be left with a handful of sad-looking flower stems. And in his more fanciful moods, Chris had often thought that flower stems minus the flowers, like dandelions without their fuzz, looked like pitiful dead things. He really didn't need that symbolism or metaphor or whatever it was today.

No, not a metaphor . . . a simile. Similes used the words "like" or "as." Metaphors just *were*.

"Anyway," he sighed, settling cross-legged in front of the gravestone that was getting so familiar it almost didn't make him want to cry. "I just wanted to . . . oh, the ground is *wet*," he said, and stood up. Luckily he hadn't soaked his pants. Chris had the definite feeling that his aunt was laughing good naturedly at him from somewhere, possibly above.

"I wish I knew how much of this you planned," Chris said, shoving his hands into his pockets and pacing awkwardly back and forth in front of the grave. It was a weird place to pace, and he wasn't sure if he was being rude to his aunt or the other people buried here, but he needed to talk to somebody and he hated the idea of forgetting Aunt Elsie. So here he was, talking to thin air the way he used to work things out by talking to his aunt. "And I wish I knew if *you* knew about the professor or not."

Because if she had, then why hadn't she *warned* Chris and Carrie? Aunt Elsie, of all people, should have known how much time Chris and Carrie spent with Professor Griffin, and that they wouldn't see a betrayal coming from him. Frankly, Chris was still having trouble dealing with what the professor had done, and he kept catching himself planning out what to tell the professor before realizing that that was now a bad idea, and at times his brain refused to believe that the past forty-eight hours had happened. He kept expecting Professor Griffin to come around a corner saying: "smaller Kingsolvers!" with absolute sincerity. "Smaller Kingsolvers" was a term of endearment used only by Professor Griffin, and the thought of never hearing it again was upsetting.

"Wait," Chris said, the phrasing of his aunt's last letter floating in front of his eyes. "Did you leave me a warning in that letter? And I just didn't see it?"

His aunt *had* addressed Chris and Carrie as "smaller Kingsolvers" in her last letter to Chris, a term which, while not exactly obscure, was pretty much exclusively Professor Griffin's term of affection.

✗ ✗ ✗

"I think she tried to warn us," Chris told Carrie that afternoon. Carrie was on the couch poking at a sandwich, and Chris was lacing his shoes. His mom was in the kitchen, muttering about the end of the world, which meant that someone had eaten all the bread-and-butter pickles.

"Who?" Carrie asked. "Maddison, or Aunt Elsie?" Chris gaped at her but she just rolled her eyes. "What? Those are the only two people who might possibly try to warn us about something!"

Chris reminded himself that Carrie was just as capable of paranoia as he was and explained that he'd meant Aunt Elsie, because she was the one who had told them to be careful about someone who was close to them. "And then she used Professor Griffin's pet name for us instead of hers," he added.

"Aunt Elsie didn't have a pet name for us," Carrie pointed out through a mouthful of turkey sandwich. "But you might be right about her trying to warn us."

"Plus, if Aunt Elsie warned us about Professor Griffin, there might be other things in that letter that we've missed?"

"True," Carrie said, "but—"

"I don't even want to know what you two are

plotting in here," Chris's mom said, framed in the doorway. "Come on, I have to go *find more pickles* and we're wasting daylight."

CHAPTER THREE

AGENT MICHELLE GREY LOOKED AT THE SHATtered remains of a boat and allowed herself a single, irritated sigh. Then she squared her shoulders and marched across the beach towards *The Vanishing Triangle,* her expression thunderous.

The Vanishing Triangle had washed up on the fifth-most-popular seashell-hunting beach on Archer's Grove sometime between apprehending Harvey Tanner and dawn. At least, that's when Detective Hermann seemed to think the ship had wrecked.

And it was . . . a mess, to be honest. The whole

scene was a mess, and a confusing and nonsensical one at that. The beach was clearly marked, the night had not been stormy, and the one dangerous rocky bit of beach was well known and easily avoided by even mediocre sailors. So, how *The Vanishing Triangle* had wound up rammed into a pile of driftwood and rocks, its hull hacked to pieces and its propeller missing, Michelle didn't know. It was almost as if—

"This ship was wrecked on purpose," Detective Hermann said when Michelle met him at the edge of the crime tape he was putting up. "At least that's what I suspect," he clarified, dusting wet sand from his hands. "I'm not declaring that the result of the investigation or anything, but at this point no one is going to complain we're wasting manpower on an act of God. This poor ship looks like someone took a *knife* to it in some places!"

"Any signs of a struggle?" Michelle asked. She didn't ask how possible it would be to find those signs on a soaking wet boat that had been thoroughly trashed. In Agent Grey's experience, if you acted like something was possible even if you didn't know if it was or not, and especially if it was generally impossible, then nine times out of ten people went off and did it for you anyway.

"We don't know yet," Detective Hermann said. He lifted the caution tape for Michelle and she ducked under and stepped carefully closer to the hull. "So far we haven't turned up any bodies or any blood, but I've got crime scene investigation coming in as soon as they get their gear together and they might turn something up," he said, then pointed to a sodden piece of heavy plastic caught in a jagged edge of broken ship. "What worries me is this."

"That's a waterproof bag," Michelle said. Boating wasn't her area of expertise, but she'd handled a few cases near the water and she had taken every emergency safety course she could. "It's not for a—"

"Emergency life raft, yeah," Detective Hermann sighed. "It is. When we found the remains of the regular lifeboat with holes stabbed in the bottom,

I thought we were going to find a body, but now I'm afraid we have Griffin loose on the island somewhere."

"Great," Michelle said, and called Forrest to tell him to put the Ryan Moore case files down and get himself, and perhaps some lunch, over to the state park, because it was turning into one of *those* cases.

Willis Griffin's graduate student turned up before Forrest did, eyes red and shoulders set and furious. Michelle felt encouraged. This did not look like someone who adored her professor and refused to so much as consider that he might have done something wrong.

"I couldn't believe it when I heard," the girl—her name was Abigail—said, twisting the cord attached to her camera around and around her thumb. She didn't even know she was doing it, and her thumb was turning blue. "I need to take"—she had to stop and blink for a moment—"I need to take a few pictures of the boat, since it belonged to the school, and s-someone from the president's office will be out here by the end of the hour, I was just closer."

"Don't cross the caution tape and you'll be fine," Michelle said, pulling a tissue out of her bag for Abigail. "And if you see anything strange or missing tell me or Detective Hermann, okay?"

Abigail nodded and wandered in the direction of the boat, which was now crawling with crime scene investigators. Michelle watched her go but startled when she turned back around to find Forrest right there. He had sandwiches, though, so she forgave him.

"Forgive me for what?" Forrest asked, producing a bottle of soda and a smaller paper bag containing muffins. In his other hand he had a bag of sandwiches and a file folder. Michelle watched him with apprehension. Forrest was a competent and quick-thinking person, but he could never balance a sandwich and a drink without dropping something.

"Where were you this morning?" Michelle took

the muffins from him before he could drop them in the wet sand.

"The entire investigation into the disappearance of Ryan Moore is a mess," Forrest said.

Michelle was in the process of casting around for a picnic table where she could park them both and ask him what he meant by the case being a mess when Abigail gave a startled yelp and came running down the beach towards them.

"I think you need to see this!" she gasped. "Someone *moved Moby*. The submersible," she added when nobody reacted in an appropriately shocked and awed manner. "Professor Griffin was supposed to be using the submersible on this trip, but *Moby* isn't on the wrecked boat anywhere!"

Instead, the submersible had been tucked neatly away under the overhang of the men's restroom, a light blue tarp tossed over it and weighed down with rocks at the four corners. One of the rocks had rolled away during the night and a corner of the tarp was waving in the breeze, which was likely the only reason Abigail had recognized *Moby*. That, and the fact that Abigail knew what *Moby was*. To Michelle, the submersible looked like nothing more than an awkward collection of hardware supplies, and even when Abigail pointed it out she couldn't really see how a camera was supposed to attach to the thing.

"It is technically removable," Abigail said, in a tone of voice that suggested that anyone who thought that removing *Moby*'s camera was a good idea was nuts, "but without his camera *Moby* isn't much use. Especially not if you wanted to study coastal erosion . . . "

"Coastal erosion?" Forrest whispered to Michelle, puzzled.

"Anyway, when I heard about Chris and Carrie I went and checked the equipment rooms," Abigail said. "He left the camera behind; that's when I knew Professor Griffin really had gone off the deep end."

"But apparently not enough that he was willing to risk *Moby* in a crash, or just leave *Moby* exposed to the elements," Forrest pointed out. "Pity there aren't any footprints."

There weren't; if Griffin had dragged *Moby* from the beach to the blacktop of the picnic and bathroom area he'd brushed out his footprints afterwards, and the bathrooms were right next to the parking lot, which led right to a major road. Michelle looked at the little submersible in irritation. There were far too many ways Griffin could have placed the submersible, covered his tracks, and fled.

"More trouble than you're worth, with more questions than answers," she told *Moby*.

"That's what Agent Grey says about everyone," Forrest told Abigail reassuringly, "she doesn't particularly hate your robot."

"He's a submersible," Abigail said, "and he's been called much, much worse."

✗ ✗ ✗

"So what did you get out of the Ryan Moore

disappearance?" Michelle said after they had sent CSI back to their labs, allowed Abigail to take her submersible back to the college (after recruiting six police officers to help her haul it into her truck), exchanged polite words with the legal representative the college had sent over, been reassured by a harassed-sounding woman that there would be a park ranger on her way to them within the hour, and sent Detective Hermann home for a nap. *That* had been when Michelle had realized he'd been up longer than everyone else by about four hours.

They were finally eating their sandwiches, parked at the picnic table and enjoying a warm summer day and sweet ocean breezes. The only thing that made it less than lovely was the crashed ship and all the caution tape, but Michelle was used to sneaking meals around crime scenes and the sandwiches and muffins Forrest had brought were far too good to worry about location.

"Not nearly as much as I should have," Forrest said, picking a large slice of tomato out of his sandwich. He only liked tomatoes in very small pieces, a fact that puzzled Michelle more than most of the strange behavior she had seen in the twenty-two years she'd been in law enforcement. "Whoever initially put the case together was doing so with their toes."

Michelle paused in the middle of biting into a muffin. That was *horrible* imagery to use while eating. "That bad, huh?" she asked, and Forrest scowled in reply.

"They practically picked a suspect out of a hat and then fit all the evidence to him—and at this point McRae could have been suspicious as all get-out and we wouldn't be able to tell, because the eyewitness reports were slanted this way and that. *Obviously* slanted this way and that," he added, and Michelle grimaced. "Nobody followed up on a side remark from Wyzowski that should have gotten more attention, especially considering what we're dealing with now, and I can't actually find any proof that the other four friends of Ryan Moore were asked to account for their movements that night. I'd like to give the detective in charge of the case a piece of my mind and throw the police chief at the time out the window!"

"Nah, believe it or not he's the only reason there wasn't a miscarriage of justice," a voice said directly behind them, and Michelle and Forrest turned around to find a short, sturdy-looking woman with tanned skin and a no-nonsense French braid studying them. If the badge and the uniform hadn't tipped them off, her very *aura* of nature would have: this was the park ranger they were expecting.

"Helen Kinney," the woman said, offering first Michelle and then Forrest her hand. "Sorry about that, I didn't mean to sneak up on you but I was checking hiking trails in the area and I came up through the back footpath." She waved a hand in the general direction of the tall grasses and trees along the rim of the parking lot. The closest parking lot, aside from this one, was some twenty miles away—and yet she didn't even seem to be breathing hard.

"No problem," Michelle said, even as she privately wondered what sort of person took that sort of hike as a matter of course. "I'm Agent Grey, this is Agent Holland. We were told someone from the park service would be out to talk with us?"

"Yep," Kinney said, settling herself at the picnic table. "I'm the senior ranger here so I'm what you get. We've got five full-time people and five seasonal, along with a rotating roster of volunteers, but I'm senior. And I've also been here the longest. I can handle any legal issues with the boat." She paused. "Or, I should say that I can give any legal issues with the boat to the right people, and I can put you in touch with the rangers on duty when this happened."

"I thought there wasn't usually a ranger in this part of the island full time?" Forrest said. *Good, he's done his homework*, Michelle thought, pleased.

"There isn't, but we try to have someone stop by every park at least once every night in the summer," Kinney explained. "Gives us a way to check for poachers, lost tourists, that sort of thing." She tapped the pen she'd produced from nowhere against the table. "Noah Bronwen was on duty last night, but he was dealing with a lost kayak for most of the evening and the sweep of this beach he did was pretty early."

"We'll still like to talk to him," Michelle said. It was hardly even a disappointment that the ranger on duty hadn't seen anything, since it was more or less the natural state of things. People very seldom happened to witness crimes being committed, even when that was what they were paid to do. *The Vanishing Triangle* had been beached and wrecked in the early morning hours with nobody to witness it, and there had already been inquisitive hermit crabs studying it when a woman out walking her dog had found it and called 911. "And what do you mean, the detective in charge of the Moore case is the only reason there wasn't a miscarriage of justice?" Michelle asked, frowning.

"Ah," Kinney said. "That."

Forrest put down the remains of his sandwich, the better to peer intently at the park ranger, who looked . . . not uncomfortable, exactly. More like faintly calculating.

"I've met the now-retired detective who handled that case," Kinney said. "Not face-to-face but we've talked before. I met him through a mutual friend who is forever finding new and exciting ways to cause himself anguish; Greg and I bonded over our mutual frustration with Kevin's tendency to go it alone."

"Was this friend Kevin McRae, by any chance?" Michelle asked.

Kinney raised one eyebrow as she nodded.

"Aargh," said Forrest.

"Things do seem to keep swinging back around to him, don't they?" Michelle said lightly, even as she despaired of ever getting a witness who didn't know three other witnesses and have strong feelings about all three. She was *never* going to get an unbiased look at the case if this kept up!

"I do understand the difficulty this causes for you," Kinney added, before Michelle could give in to the temptation to bang her head against the table. "For what it's worth, I can provide you with a half-dozen character witnesses for myself and I can arrange for someone else to liaise with you if it causes you too much trouble."

"No, that'll be fine," Michelle said faintly. "The next person will most likely turn out to be Griffin's second cousin twice removed."

"As far as I know he doesn't have any family, at least not in the area," Kinney said. "There might be a mother on mainland Florida."

Michelle wasn't sure if that proved her point, or gave her useful information about a person of interest, or both. And she didn't really have time to ask, either, because then Kinney got a call about possible smugglers. "Or it could just be someone with engine trouble, you never can tell in that neck of the cypress swamp," she said, and stood to go do her job.

"You should know, though," she added before she marched back into the woods, having waved off an offer from Forrest to drive her to her car with the assurance that she knew where she was going, and admitting that she needed the time to clear her head before dealing with someone named DeWinter, "that Lyndon retired not long after the Moore case was shelved, and that he still considers it his worst failure." She fixed Michelle with a *look*, and added, "Because he could never figure out why his department went nuts on him and he could never find the source of the corruption."

Without being asked, Forrest pulled some strings and got his hands on the personnel files for everyone involved in the Moore case by the time Michelle was done chasing down worthless leads and finding something resembling dinner. And what he found was frankly baffling.

Of the detectives assigned to the case, not one had had prior experience. The officers who responded to the initial call were not the officers who handled any of the following investigation. The lab work—such that it was, there wasn't much from the crime scene, or at least not much that was *tested*—was sent to a laboratory out of state, which lost the samples. And aside from Lyndon, who had been the police chief at the time and seemed to be a generally sensible and levelheaded person, none of the individuals involved in the case had even gone on to collect retirement. It was truly as if the entire police department had gone completely insane for the span of one case and then, through a series of reassignments, firings, and moves out of state, the major players had all disappeared.

"Stranger and stranger," Michelle grumbled to herself, and went in search of retired detective Gregory Lyndon's phone number.

CHAPTER FOUR

AUNT ELSIE'S HOUSE HAD BEEN UNTOUCHED since her funeral. Since before her funeral, really, in that aside from her brothers fetching the few things they needed *for* the funeral and certain arrangements after her death, nobody had been in the house since she'd left it one morning and not come back.

Chris wished he could get that thought out of his mind, but he couldn't. He had always loved Aunt Elsie's house, an old Georgian mansion draped with Spanish moss and a hundred times more meaning- ful and impressive a structure than his own box of a family home. True, the general consensus was that if Aunt Elsie's house wasn't haunted itself then the woods behind it had to be, but to Chris that had always been a draw, not a reason to stay away. He was not going to let his own personal ghosts keep him away when a real ghost couldn't.

"Real ghost?" Maddison asked, peering up at the big dark windows as Chris's mom's car crunched down the gravel drive away from them. Chris's mom had, true to her word, picked up Maddison and then dropped them all off at Aunt Elsie's house before heading back into town to go shopping. That they had been followed at a discreet distance by Officer Carson was only slightly awkward, but had been a nonnegotiable point for Chris's mom. And Maddison's dad.

The police officer had, at least, walked around the house once to check for obvious signs of forced entry, and then announced that unless they really wanted him to join them, he would be staying outside in his cruiser and keeping an eye on everything from there, so at least Chris didn't have to worry about trying to look through Aunt Elsie's papers while a police officer watched.

"It's a very old house," Chris explained. "A couple of people have died in it, and people *say* at least one of them was murdered."

"You ever seen a ghost in there?" Maddison asked.

Chris looked up at his aunt's house, willed to him when he turned twenty-one, and frowned. "The doors in that house have never stayed closed the way they should," he admitted. "But Carrie will just say that's just . . ."

"Because it's a very old house made of wood, and we are in Florida, and humidity is a thing that exists," Carrie obligingly finished for Chris, although she had a point. Chris had never felt even the remotest bit unnerved by his aunt's house before, and the creepy feeling that was making the hairs on the back of his neck stand up right now was in no way, shape, or form caused by a ghost. Chris cast one last nervous look at the front of the house, and then marched purposely for the porch and the front door, fishing the key out of his pocket as he did so.

His first overwhelming impression once he got the door open was something along the lines of "Help, stuffy." The air conditioning had actually been left on very low, because Aunt Elsie had provided for doing so in her will. She had too many fragile personal papers and had spent too much time as an archivist to trust that the papers she had left to different people would get to them in a timely manner, so the house was to be kept minimally climate controlled for the sake of the papers. It was the archivist in her coming out with a vengeance, and it meant that the house wasn't as bad as it could have been. Still, nobody had been in the house in weeks and the air was stale and dusty as they trooped in the front door and meandered their way through the front parlor and into the kitchen.

"Gah," Carrie said, wrinkling her nose. "I realize it's a little late to be asking this question, but where did the papers end up, anyway?"

"I don't remember?" Chris offered. "I was really upset, and kind of panicking about Maddison's dad."

"Gee, thanks."

"And about what Aunt Elsie left me in her letter," Chris offered. "I let Mom take the boxes and put them up here. Somewhere." He spun in a circle, frowning. The most logical place to put the boxes would have been the kitchen table, which was instead empty except for a thin layer of dust. Carrie hummed thoughtfully under her breath and wandered out of the kitchen and on into the rest of the house. Maddison, either because she felt uncomfortable or because she simply had no idea how the house was laid out, was following Chris so closely they were almost bumping into each other.

"Hey, did your mom maybe come in through the back door?" Carrie called from the back study. "Because I found—okay, yeah, it's back here!"

"Why did she come in through the back door?" Chris asked, following his cousin's voice to the little blue-painted study with two large windows that looked out over the side garden, which was currently a riot of overgrown weeds and vegetables. There were three ground-level doors to Aunt Elsie's house. One, of course, was the front door, but then there was also a sliding-glass door in the kitchen, and a difficult door that was forever getting stuck in the back of the house that was almost next to the study. There was also a door in the upstairs hallway that opened into thin air, but that one Aunt Elsie had wired closed years ago so a small Chris and Carrie couldn't accidentally open it. Because it opened onto a sheer drop, unless you had wings or a ladder it wasn't a good way to get into the house.

"Because the driveway loops around the house?" Carrie suggested, but her attention was focused more on the cardboard boxes that had been dumped unceremoniously on the floor of Aunt Elsie's office than on Chris's confusion over their being *there*. Giving up on that train of thought, Chris dropped to his knees next to the largest of the boxes, Maddison following his lead. It looked as though Chris's mom had simply carried all five boxes in, dropped them in the office, and left without bothering to open or organize anything, and it had been several weeks since Chris and Carrie had cleared out their aunt's office at the Archive. Everything was exactly as Chris had packed it, but by this point he couldn't remember what he packed where. For several minutes the only sounds in the room were the sounds of three people sifting through stacks of papers, looking for anything that wasn't spare stationary, emergency flooding procedures, or records-disposal schedules.

"Why did the Archive do a records-disposal schedule for the college almost twice a year?" Carrie muttered when she'd neared the bottom of the first box, and Chris looked up from the box he was sifting through and pointed out that if the number of years you legally needed to keep records changed, then that was the sort of thing you needed to keep track of.

"I know that," Carrie grumbled, "but what does the Archive have to do with the college?"

"Was your aunt doing extra stuff for the college?" Maddison asked.

"Probably," Chris answered absently. Aunt Elsie had done a lot of archives consulting for the area, whenever an organization that couldn't afford a full-time archivist had called her in to sort through their stuff and tell them what they should be saving and what they didn't need to keep. Aunt Elsie had called it going through the dirty laundry without the embarrassment for all sides that going through the dirty laundry usually included—unless, she had added once, after Chris and Carrie had turned fifteen and she had decided they could be told the less flattering things about life—you happened to stumble across evidence that the president of the relief fund was embezzling money. Then it just got terribly awkward and you ended up not being able to finish the job because some people prided the good name of the organization over the truth. Aunt Elsie had been thoroughly irritated, even though the incident had, as far as Chris and Carrie had been able to tell, happened when they were three.

"Well"—Carrie made several impressive faces before sneezing violently—"if nothing else, Aunt Elsie was interested in the college's records-disposal schedule; there are, like, twenty-five of them in here. And none of them are copies, either," she added, and then sneezed again.

"I've got nothing but general office supplies stuff," Maddison admitted, holding up a package of highlighters. "And a whole stack of sticky notes with notes taken on them that were then stuck back together in a pad?"

"Oh, Aunt Elsie did that all the time," Carrie said. "Sometimes she did little flip books when she was bored, see, look—" She took the pad of pink sticky notes from Maddison and dragged her thumb along the side. On the sticky note pad, a little stick figure ran across the bottom of the page and then did a little dance.

Chris left them to it. There was something

tugging at the edge of his memory, and it had to do with the boxes. He'd been very upset when he'd packed most of this stuff—he honestly hadn't noticed the sticky note flip books when he'd been turning out drawers—and then Dr. McRae had turned up and made the whole situation even more complicated and awkward. But there was something . . .

Chris unfolded the flaps from the largest and least full box. If his spotty memory of that terrible day was right, it had been the box he was filling when Dr. McRae wandered into Chris's life and accidentally triggered Chris's "serial-killer" vibes. The box was mostly full of file folders, and most of them weren't even full themselves, but as he lifted out the second-largest handful of folders, something in the bottom made a clicking, pinging sort of noise. Like the metal rings of a three-ring binder snagging on the box.

"Wait a second," Chris whispered, and almost fell into the overly large box in his quest to fish out the three-ring binder that he'd stuffed in there without a second glance weeks ago. It still had a strip of duct tape sealing it closed, and it still said "*The*" on the front in Aunt Elsie's handwriting.

Unless, Chris thought, stretching out the leg that was beginning to go all pins and needles from his sitting on it too long, *Aunt Elsie wrote the letters while a little rushed or a lot distracted, when her normally legible hand got sloppy.* Then it was just possible for the E to look like a C, or rather for the C to look like an E, which would mean—

"Treasure Hunters Club," Chris said out loud, and Carrie and Maddison both turned as one to look at him. Chris held up the binder.

"THE?" Maddison said.

"THC?" Carrie said.

"I didn't look at this when I pulled it out of Aunt Elsie's desk," Chris explained. He started trying to pick the tape off. It had been stretched tightly across the binder, and the gummy but still-glued-down edges suggested that it had been years since the tape had been disturbed. "Maddison's dad turned up right as I was doing it and he freaked me out so badly that I just shoved everything into a box and didn't . . . " He trailed off, feeling guilty. He'd been so sure, when Dr. McRae turned up out of nowhere that day, that *he* was the person behind his aunt's untimely death. Most likely, Dr. McRae had been poking around the Archive that day trying to figure out what *Professor Griffin* was up to. It was more than a little horrifying to realize that Chris had gotten the motivations of the two men completely mixed up.

"You didn't stop to think about what was in the binder because you were too busy suspecting my dad of funny business?" Maddison offered, but she sounded more faintly amused than mad.

"I'd still like to know what he was trying to *find* that day," Chris said, picking at the duct tape. "I mean, if I'd asked him would he have tried to warn me away from Professor Griffin?"

"I think he just wanted to meet you," Maddison

said honestly. "And see Aunt Elsie's office. He said something about her having sent him a postcard not long before she"—Maddison paused and looked around the shuttered house—"died. I *think* Dad was a lot more shaken up by losing Aunt Elsie than he likes to admit. And anyway," she added, "if you actually had asked him any questions, he probably would've panicked and jumped out a window or something, he's really, really bad about explaining stuff like this."

"You got *something* out of him," Carrie pointed out.

"Mr. Lyndon locked us in a room together," Maddison explained. "What's in the folder?"

"Let's see," said Chris, and he ripped the duct tape off. It did not want to come quietly. He ended up wrestling with sticky strands and ripping the edges of some of the papers in the binder, which was so fat with paper that the plastic-covered cardboard edges didn't touch each other. Some of the duct tape was glued to the paper either way, but at least Chris managed not to rip any papers all the way out. "I really have no idea what's in here," Chris admitted while he unstuck the last of the tape. "I'm only going off this weird feeling that Aunt Elsie wanted this hidden. Aside from the tamper-proof duct tape seal, when I was cleaning out her desk I found this binder under a folder the exact same color as the rest of the desk."

"You mean the folder that's almost twice as big as the other folders," Carrie said from inside the box. "The same color as Aunt Elsie's desk, and completely and entirely empty except for a sheet of printer paper with the words 'test page' on it?"

"Yeah," Chris said, and then, "huh," because he'd finally disposed of the tape and opened the folder.

"Well?" Carrie said.

"It's meeting minutes," Chris said, bewildered. The papers were regular, loose-leaf, college-rule notebook paper, and the very first one was nothing but a series of almost-cryptic notes in his aunt's hand, listing the number of suggested votes for president, secretary, vice president, and backup–vice president.

"W.G. suggested electing officers," Chris read, frowning, "but was outvoted by R.W. and K.G., who both refuse to make this club any more official than it already is. R.M. and E.K. seconded the motion and assigned offices based on intensity levels." Chris stopped. "This is a record of Aunt Elsie and Professor Griffin's college treasure hunting," he said, shocked.

"And my dad," Maddison said, wide eyed. "Keep going, who got elected to what position?"

"Um." Chris squinted at the page. His aunt had been a brief note-taker, so everything was in the form of neat bullet points and short phrases, a homegrown shorthand that Chris could only sort of figure out after years of reading his aunt's shopping lists. She'd also only used initials, and while it was not impossible to figure out that W.G. was Willis Griffin, R.M. was Ryan Moore, and E.K. was Elsie Kingsolver, Chris wasn't sure who R.W. and K.G. were.

"It looks like they appointed Ryan Moore president, Willis Griffin vice president, K.G. backup–vice president, and then Aunt Elsie appointed herself secretary," Chris said.

"K.G. is my dad," Maddison said. "My dad took my mom's last name—McRae—when they got married," she explained when Chris and Carrie turned to look at her. "But back then his last name was Greenwood. So I'm sure the K.G. is Kevin Greenwood."

"So R.W.?" Carrie asked.

"Well that's—" Something creaked outside, and everyone froze.

"Oh no, not again," Carrie moaned, dropping to the floor and glancing frantically for cover. Chris followed her example a second later, as did Maddison. The windows in Aunt Elsie's office were set high enough in the wall that sitting around the boxes on the floor *should* have prevented them from being seen by anyone.

"Do you hear something?" Maddison hissed from

her position almost under Aunt Elsie's desk. Chris strained his ears to hear. Carrie was stifling a sneeze after all the dust they'd stirred up.

"You mean do I hear a faint squeaking sound that might be someone trying to get the sliding-glass door in the kitchen to open?" Carrie whispered. She sniffed furiously. Her eyes were starting to get red, too—if they didn't leave soon she was heading into breaking-into-hives territory. "Yes, and I wish I didn't!"

"I think it's more of a scraping sound," Chris said, and there was really no reason for both Carrie and Maddison to fix him with such completely disdainful looks. "Well, it is!" Chris protested, clutching the binder full of meeting notes tightly to his chest and wondering why someone was trying to get in through the kitchen door, especially when they had left the front door unlocked on their way in. Except that the kitchen door was the only one you could sneak up to from the woods, since it was on the opposite side of the house from the driveway, so if, say, you were trying to stay out of sight from the road but still needed to get into the house . . . and that *might* mean that you walked in from somewhere else, and didn't know what the driveway looked like, and so *didn't* know that there was a police car parked in the driveway . . .

Carefully as possible, Chris slid his phone out of his pocket. His mom had made him put Officer Carson's number in his emergency contacts list, and for once he had cell service. Time to see if whoever was trying to get into the house wanted to deal with the police.

✗ ✗ ✗

As it most anticlimactically turned out, they didn't.

"Whoever it was is *fast*," Officer Carson gasped, leaning against the side of his cruiser and panting for breath. "And they must know the land better than I do."

"Did you see who it was?" Carrie asked. Officer

Carson had answered Chris on the second ring, and then ordered him, Carrie, and Maddison to stay right where they were and to stay *down,* and circled the house after whoever was trying to get in the door. Chris had heard the officer shout, "Freeze!" followed by a couple of words Officer Carson's mother probably wouldn't approve of, and then nothing until the now-winded police officer had knocked on the door to tell them that it was safe for the moment.

"No." Officer Carson grimaced. "I didn't see who it was. I saw a white male with his back to me who did *not* drop the metal pry-bar in his hands before booking it into the woods when he heard me."

"That's a good way to describe half our suspect pool," Maddison said. Officer Carson looked at her in surprise for a second, then heaved a resigned sigh and stopped using the police cruiser to prop himself up.

"I'm not even going to comment," he said with a sigh. "Except for how I am. I don't know if you three found what you came for or not, but I can't have you here while we have a possible suspect on the loose in the area."

So they were ushered into the police cruiser, which was more than a bit of a tight fit. Then Officer Carson insisted on making sure that Maddison was inside her house and that the officer parked in her neighbor's driveway was aware of the newest developments in the case before he left, and then he had to do the same for Carrie, and then he walked Chris all the way to the door and checked the house before he left Chris inside.

"Nobody has been back here since your mother left to go grocery shopping," Officer Carson explained when Chris started to wonder if this was overkill. "And according to your mother, Willis Griffin had a key to your house."

Well, okay, so it probably wasn't overkill.

But then finally Chris was left alone, and with Aunt Elsie's treasure-hunting-club notes. He locked all the doors first, and then built a pyramid of tin cans in front of the front and back doors and wedged a chair under his own doorknob. It probably wouldn't stop a really determined Professor Griffin but it might slow him down and give Chris time to go out the window.

Speaking of which—*that* he left unlocked, just in case. Then, and only then, did Chris sit down at his desk and open his aunt's notebook and start from the beginning.

CHAPTER FIVE

SHE HAD STARTED BY TAKING HER SELF-APPOINTED secretary duties very seriously. The first ten neatly dated pages Chris read were, quite frankly, boring; they were simple bullet-pointed lists of what had been discussed during the meeting: W.G. presented research on *San Telmo*; W.G. presented a slideshow of beaches where solid gold coins from the 1717 fleet had washed up; R.M. found a history of the 1717 fleet in *Great Ships of the Ocean*—Chris paused to look that title up and was only slightly surprised to find that it was out of print, not available on Amazon, and marked as "missing" in his local library's catalog.

"R.W. proposes alien involvement" was apparently the point at which Aunt Elsie had stopped taking her duties seriously, since beside that bullet point she had written in the margin "no, really" and drawn a classic gray (with big black eyes, a tiny body, an abnormally large head, and a silhouette that just generally screamed 'alien,' it was hard to mistake, plus she'd shaded it gray in pencil) wearing a party hat.

"But who is R.W.?" Chris asked aloud, and turned the page. After that, it appeared as if Aunt Elsie had started using her note taking as a way to amuse herself during meetings. There were little doodles in the corners of the pages, amusing comments, even a history essay outlined on the back of the meeting minutes for the November of Aunt Elsie's junior year. The only thing Chris didn't find, as he read his aunt's notes on treasure hunting, the reliability of metal detectors, and the danger of using a metal detector while your friends were sitting under a sun umbrella with a metal handle right next to you, was anyone's full name.

If you knew Professor Griffin, it was easy enough to tell that W.G. was the person whose semester-long battle of wills with an English professor over the correct interpretation of the white whale in *Moby-Dick* was chronicled by Aunt Elsie in the meeting minutes. If you had met Dr. McRae, you could start to see him in K.G.'s quick ability to spin a story and his interest in Spanish mission churches. Ryan Moore was a cypher and a skeleton in a cistern to Chris, but he had apparently been a bright, friendly, handsome sort, who let everyone else chatter away and then came out with completely unexpected and entirely new ideas that led you in entirely new directions just when you least expected them.

R.W., though, was a complete mystery. He was a bit of an oddball, that much was apparent from almost the first meeting notes. He was fond of ghosts and scary stories, he liked the outdoors, he had a flair for the dramatic that sometimes left his grades to suffer, and he was cheerfully convinced that aliens were a viable theory in the disappearance of a Spanish treasure ship. Honestly, Chris thought he sounded like an interesting person to get to know, although aliens were a bit much even for Chris.

Chris flipped a page. "Oh," he said. "Now he thinks it's Atlantis." To be fair, mythical underwater cities were a slightly better explanation for missing ships than aliens, seeing as they shared the element of water. *Although aliens have ships*, Chris thought. *So technically they could be oceangoing and we might never know, considering how big the ocean is.* And hadn't he read something about Atlantis being related to aliens in one of the books he'd borrowed from Maddison? Chris put a bookmark in the meeting notes and switched his computer on—a terrible idea, since when he next looked up it was to realize that he'd spent almost two hours reading increasingly confusing theories about how extraterrestrial beings, and *extradimensional* beings, were responsible for the creation of Atlantis. They were also allegedly behind a lot of Bigfoot sightings. "I don't think Bigfoot is extradimensional," Chris told his computer, which of course didn't have an opinion one way or another.

What he was really doing was stalling, because three and a half years of once-a-month meeting notes were a lot of meeting notes, and as fascinating as it was to read page after page of his aunt's quiet observations, Chris was getting both bored and frustrated. He needed to find something that might tell him what Professor Griffin would do when all his plans fell apart, or how his aunt expected him to find the *San Telmo* when the coordinates didn't work, or who R.W. was, not a detailed floor map of the mythical Atlantis.

Plus, Chris still had the maddening feeling about the initials R.W. It was on the very tip of his tongue, and plowing through all these meeting notes was taking time he didn't have. It was enough to make someone wish for an index at the back of the book! Chris actually liked indexes and glossaries, for the simple reason that they cut down on the amount of time you spent trying and failing to read carefully through the whole book looking for a particular term so you could see what the book said about it. Carrie called this cheating, but Chris usually argued that not everyone was as good at taking notes while reading homework assignments the first time. But unfortunately hand-written and hand-collected books didn't usually have indexes. What sort of person would go to that much trouble? Or know how to make an index that wasn't a tangled mess?

Chris froze, grabbed that thought, and yanked it into the light so he could look at it more closely. Then he flipped the whole three-ring binder over so he could look at the very back. What kind of person would have both the knowledge and the inclination to put an index at the back of a book? Well, an archivist, for one.

There wasn't an index, exactly. For one thing, the pages in the binder weren't numbered, so an index would be hard to put together. But in the back of her notebook Aunt Elsie *had* written down the dates the notes covered, in chronological order, and then she had included a key to the abbreviations she used regularly:

H2O = Water

+ = and

A.E. = Amelia Island

S.T. = *San Telmo*

A.G. = Archer's Grove

K.G. = Kevin Greenwood

W.G. = Willis Griffin

E.K. = Elsie Kingsolver

R.M. = Ryan Moore

R.W. = Robin Wyzowski

Chris stared at the last name on the list and felt the bottom of his stomach drop out. Robin Wyzowski was the one person in his aunt's treasure-hunting club who hadn't popped out of the woodwork and caused confusing problems for Chris and Carrie, except Robin Wyzowski was the name Robin Redd had been born with, which meant that he'd been there all along and never told anyone. And Redd—Wyzowski—whatever—had ducked out of talking to the police. Was he hiding something? Or rather, was he hiding *from* someone? What if Redd had been less worried about missing filming than about being recognized? And come to think of it, why *had* Redd been filming so conveniently in the same place Chris and Carrie went overboard? Why had he told them his real name—had he been trying to see how much they knew? Was his being in the woods at the exact same time Chris and Carrie and Maddison were looking for the lost mission church really a coincidence, or was that simply what Redd wanted everyone to think?

And why on Earth had Chris's dad and uncle never bothered to mention that Aunt Elsie knew the host of *Robin Redd: Treasure Hunter*? Well, actually, that one could be easily explained away by their not wanting to bring shame on the family name, but still! Who did Robin Redd think he was?

✗ ✗ ✗

Robin Wyzowski, better known to the general public as Robin Redd, stood in the cemetery in the dying light of a gorgeous summer sunset, a bouquet of flowers in his hands. "I'm a fool," he said.

The bouquet was one of the larger types, stuffed full of flowers that grew at all different times of the year and quite expensive, and he'd gotten an odd look from the florist when he asked especially for Michaelmas daisies. He'd offered that they were also commonly called asters and she'd explained that they weren't normally a popular flower. She'd had to add them in, and had grumbled in bewilderment about unexpected flower fads.

"I mean," Robin continued, setting the bouquet down on a grave already scattered with daisies and graced with a woven crown of clover, "it isn't like I haven't accepted the fact that I'm a fool, or that I don't seem to be stuck in the role no matter which way I try to escape, or that it isn't an integral part of my stage persona." He paused. He didn't seem at all phased by the presence of a clover crown or scattered daisies. "Not that I'm entirely sure what people mean by *that*, but the point apparently still stands. I'm a fool. And I'm about to do something terribly foolish and I might actually end up getting myself killed or arrested, but it's this or let myself be a fool and a coward." He leaned forward and gave the headstone a squeeze. "Elsie, you deserve more than that. You deserved more than a headstone covered with flowers," he added angrily. "Your legacy isn't supposed to be a fad for Michaelmas daisies."

When he turned and walked away, down the gravel path that wound gracefully through the cemetery and toward the rental car parked just inside the gates, it was with angry tears in his eyes.

"Wait, what?" Maddison said.

"Robin Wyzowski is Robin Redd, and I don't know whose side he's on!" Chris nearly yelled into the phone. "I *knew* there was something familiar about that 'W' name you couldn't quite remember, and then I found a key at the back of Aunt Elsie's notebook and she listed all the abbreviations she used and R.W. stood for Robin Wyzowski!"

"Yeah, I know," Maddison said.

"So we have to—wait, what?"

"I know R.W. stands for Robin Wyzowski," Maddison said. Even though they were on the phone, Chris was pretty sure she was frowning at him. "At least, I know Robin Wyzowski was friends with my dad in college. My dad already . . . told me . . . " She trailed off. "Aw, jeez, I completely forgot!"

"Your dad told you?" Chris asked. "Your dad told you that Robin Redd used to be Robin Wyzowski?" He thought they were on the same page, but they were maybe not on the same paragraph of that page.

"No," Maddison said. "Neither of us knew Robin

Redd changed his name from Wyzowski when he went into show business—although I think Dad kinda suspected—that puts a whole new and extra strange spin on things."

"Right," Chris said, catching on.

"And then everything with the ship and Professor Griffin happened, and then you and Carrie were all right, and then we were looking for more papers, and I just sort of forgot that I hadn't told *you* everything that Dad told *me!*"

"So, he already told you to be careful about Redd?"

"No?" Maddison said. "He didn't say anything at all about Redd! He told me to be careful about Professor Griffin—which was like telling me to lock the barn doors after the cows have stampeded, because at that point you were already out on the water with him and I couldn't reach you because there was no reception!"

"Phone jammer," Chris interrupted.

"What?"

"Professor Griffin had a phone jammer running on the boat," Chris explained. "That's why we weren't getting any calls."

"Well, that answers at least one of my questions," Maddison said irritably. "But Chris, Dad didn't say anything about being *suspicious* of—of Robin Redd, or Wyzowski—" She broke off, then said, "Well, you didn't!"

"Huh?" Chris asked.

"Sorry, that last bit was for my dad. He just walked in the room," Maddison explained. Then she must have muffled the phone because it sounded faint. "No, Chris just found out that Robin Redd was the Robin Wyzowski his aunt mentioned in her meeting notes—because apparently that Robin Wyzowski guy, who was the only person to make the connection between Ryan Moore's disappearance and the *San Telmo* you guys were looking for, *also happens to be Robin Redd, the television star*—what? Yes, apparently she kept those."

Maddison was one of those people who had never

figured out how to have a conversation with someone while on the phone, and her solution was to try to talk normally to both the person on the phone and the person in the room with her.

"Ask your dad if Redd might be working with Griffin," Chris said. Dr. McRae might not want to answer at all, but he was right there and it couldn't hurt to try. Maddison sighed a very put-upon sigh over the phone line and then said something to her dad that Chris couldn't quite hear.

"He says he has no idea," Maddison said. There was mumbling from the other end of the phone. "Well, that's what it sounded like!" Maddison complained, and then there was a sharp burst of static and the sound of the phone being fumbled.

"Hello?" Chris asked.

"I put you on speaker," Maddison said grimly. "Dad?"

"I didn't hear from anyone I was friends with in college, with the single exception of your aunt, after Ryan disappeared," Dr. McRae said. "However, that being said, Robin was much less paranoid and suspicious than Willis ever was, so if he's decided to ally himself with Griffin I'll be very surprised."

"Then why is he turning up everywhere we are?" Chris asked. "Professor Griffin had the old-family-friend excuse, it was normal for him to be around all the time."

"Redd turned up everywhere you were?" Dr. McRae sounded faintly horrified. "And you *didn't* get eaten by alligators or have a Civil War cannon land on your head?"

"Well, there was that whole 'getting lost at sea' thing," Maddison pointed out.

"Robin attracts leaky boats . . . "

"He could have been the person trying to get into Aunt Elsie's house this afternoon," Chris said stubbornly, still not willing to write Robin Redd off so easily. Dr. McRae seemed to think he was harmless and familiar, but Chris had thought Professor Griffin was harmless and familiar right up until the professor let him go over the side of the ship to almost certain doom.

"Redd can actually pick locks," Dr. McRae said. "Which . . . "

"Would make our intruder most likely Professor Griffin," Maddison finished. Which was when Chris's phone started beeping to let him know that he had another call.

"Chris!" Carrie said after Chris made brief excuses to Maddison and her dad, and hung up on them. "Somebody just tried to break into Professor Griffin's house."

There were any number of ways Chris could have responded—hysterical laughter sounded really tempting—but instead Chris just said, "What?" for about the third time that night.

"I've got a police cruiser parked right under my window," Carrie said grumpily. "I think Mom may have told the officer about my habit of going out the bedroom window or something, but that just means

I can hear the police radio really clearly. Since I have my window open."

Chris took a minute to reflect that Carrie's increased level of paranoia was probably in several ways his fault, and to feel quite a bit guilty about it. Then he ran what Carrie had actually said back through his mind and almost choked.

"Somebody broke into Professor Griffin's *house*? Why?"

"I don't know! Maybe they thought it was time *he* had his privacy invaded and his house ransacked!"

"Actually it's not a half-bad idea," Chris admitted.

"*No!*"

"I wasn't going to suggest we break into his house," Chris said, cringing a little at the volume Carrie had managed over the phone. "But, you know, if we wanted to drop by his office tomorrow . . ."

"Oh no," Carrie groaned. "That actually makes sense."

"It does?" Chris asked. "I mean, of course it does!"

"You're not fooling anybody."

"I need to call Maddison and her dad back," Chris said. "And, um, guess what? I figured out who R.W. is . . ."

✕ ✕ ✕

Agent Michelle Grey had lost her eye in the process of taking down an illegal parrot-smuggling operation running out of Cleveland, Ohio. She'd been a very young cop at the time, and the animal control officer who'd been on the case as well had taken her under her wing; one of the woman's favorite bits of advice was, "It can always get weirder." Michelle had argued, from her hospital bed, that there were few things weirder than losing an eye in a parrot-smuggling case. June had dropped a bag of foil-wrapped chocolate eyeballs on Michelle's bed and shook her head.

"Someday, you're going to look back on this case and think, 'Wow, that was actually one of the least complicated cases I've ever worked,' and it will be true," she had said. "You can't see it now, but this case this early on in your career is doing you a huge favor. The higher your tolerance level for weirdness, the better you'll be at finding the actual case under the . . ." She had trailed off thoughtfully.

"Parrots?" Michelle had offered.

"Exactly," June had said. "Want an eyeball?"

June had been right, although it had taken Michelle years to learn the truth of her words and how scant a comfort that advice could be. Just because she wasn't fazed by a formerly cold murder case with possible supernatural elements and way too many players didn't mean she wanted to deal with it!

Unfortunately, life never asked if you wanted to deal with formerly cold murder cases with possible supernatural elements and way too many players, it just threw them at you and left.

"Somebody tried to break into Griffin's house,"

Michelle said, head in her hands. Detective Hermann looked just as bewildered-edging-into-exasperated as she did.

"Yes," he said miserably, "and that person was Robin Redd. Or, well, we caught him in the flower beds, so we can't exactly prove that he was aiming to get inside the house. He might have been in the midst of leaving, or just admiring the moon and not looking where he was going."

"Admiring the moon and not looking where he was going?"

"That would be the explanation he gave the officer who caught him in the flower beds," Detective Hermann sighed. "And, unfortunately, as far as it goes his story checks out. The moon is nearly full tonight and there's no cloud cover, and the woman who came to get him told us he does wander around admiring the moon at night."

"I see," Michelle said. It had been a day of strange developments in the case: first there had been the discovery of *The Vanishing Triangle,* deliberately washed up on the beach and with the treasured submersible safely tucked away out of danger; then Officer Carson had reported someone trying to break into Elsie Kingsolver's house; and then Forrest had finished his digging and come to the alarming conclusion that everyone who'd handled the disappearance of Ryan Moore had since managed to expire.

Michelle knew she was looking at one murder committed over the course of this long-dormant case, and suspected she was looking at two to three, and was more than a little afraid that she was looking at practically a spree. Of particular interest was the fact that of the police officers who had worked on the Moore case, one had gone fishing and fallen from his boat, and one had been in a tragic and fatal hit-and-run accident. Car accidents and boating accidents were suspiciously common in this case.

"Yes, that's something I noticed too," Gregory Lyndon had said when Michelle managed to get in touch with him. He did not waste time or mess around—he suggested Skype rather than a phone call and had demanded to see her badge before he relaxed. Sensible, although as far as Michelle could tell the idiot who had been going around Archer's Grove pretending to be an FBI agent had in fact done the sensible thing and left as soon as he realized Michelle and Forrest were in the area.

Michelle had liked Gregory Lyndon almost immediately. It was so nice to see someone else taking paranoid precautions in the face of a very suspicious number of deaths. And the retired chief thought the deaths were suspicious, too.

"Tyler and Peter were decent cops, as far as I could tell," Lyndon had explained, "but at the time we were seriously understaffed and I had to pull people in from the next jurisdiction just to have enough guys to keep the peace. It was a college town right before finals week, the rent-a-cops they had on campus were overworked as it was, and we were patrolling fraternities," he sighed. "And somewhere in the midst of all that, someone made dang sure Ryan Moore was never found."

"Fourtrees isn't the closest place you could pull officers from," Michelle pointed out. "Was there a reason?"

"Politics, mainly," Lyndon said. "It was an election year, for one, and then the school was already on uneasy footing with the rest of the town. There was something going on between the mayor and the dean of students that I didn't like but couldn't do anything about—I don't even know what they were doing, I never got to the bottom of that—and Fourtrees had an excellent track record as far as the police department went. You'll notice, though, that none of the people we got from Fourtrees were long-time local officers." He paused, and fixed Michelle with an intense, meaningful stare. "You'll also notice," he said, "that one of the city council members in Fourtrees was a Griffin."

Michelle hissed.

"Sadly, she passed away not long ago. It was

entirely natural, and I *did* prod people into check-ing," he explained. "So of course nobody can ask her what happened in Fourtrees. And the city council records were destroyed in a freak flooding accident three years ago. But it raises some interesting questions about the investigation, doesn't it?" Lyndon asked.

"It just doesn't give *me* much to go on," Michelle said. They'd exchanged a little more information after that, none of which was really any help in *proving* anything, but just as they signed off, Lyndon had thanked her for her work and mentioned, offhand-edly, that he might have something more for her, "if the wording allows me to share it."

✕ ✕ ✕

Normally, Bethy Bradlaw was about as terrifying as a small kitten. Even in extreme anger she didn't look scary so much as she looked red and frazzled, and her main weapon of choice was paperwork. She frustrated people into going away; she didn't pop up and scare them. But every once in a while, kittens decided to turn into lions and mice decided to roar and Bethy Bradlaw seriously contemplated murder and everyone could read it in her eyes. Tonight was one of those times.

"You broke. Into the house. Of the psychopathic sea captain?" Bethy demanded. Redd gulped. Bethy was wearing floral pajamas and a large Florida Gators hoodie and her hair was loose and still damp from the shower she'd taken right before bed. She looked significantly more intimidating, at least to Redd, than the two police officers who had dropped him off after giving him a stern warning about wandering into other people's flower beds in the middle of the night.

"He's an oceanography professor," Redd said nervously. "The sea captaining is only when he has the time, and I didn't get a chance to give him a psychology test, so I don't like to throw around the label 'psychopathic' without cause . . ."

"Robin Redd," Bethy growled, "if you don't stop being cryptic I'm going to stop pretending you were here with me looking at possible shooting locations half the evening when the police want to know if you could have broken into a house!"

"Err," said Redd.

"What were you *doing*, anyway?" Bethy asked. "First that funny business with the police, then you almost scared that poor park ranger out of her skin, and now you're breaking into people's houses? I can't deal with you *and* Harry losing it at the same time, Redd!"

She was still a little angry about the Grey Cove shoot, which had devolved into chaos by the time she finally got there. Redd had overheard one park ranger talking to another about a boat washing up on shore and had nearly jumped down the poor woman's throat demanding details. Bethy had been fully prepared to make good on her threats to stuff Redd's beloved hat into a paper shredder, but he'd finally backed off and she'd let it go. And now he was up to more shenanigans and had the gall to look woeful when he got caught!

"Griffin and I knew each other at school," Redd admitted while Bethy was taking a breath in preparation for more yelling, which at least served to make Bethy stop in her half-hysterical rant. "We were . . . friends, in college, and I can't help feeling like this is my fault. I never saw this side of the man when I was eating lunch with him every day."

"That's hardly your fault," Bethy said, deflating. "But you can't go around breaking into people's houses even if you do think they pushed someone overboard."

"And those Kingsolver kids . . . " Redd said, fidgeting, "I knew their aunt too. Also in school. So it's not just that Griffin pushed them off the boat it's that Elsie died recently and Griffin might have done something to *her*, and now he's going after her niece and nephew."

Bethy blinked. "Robin," she said slowly, as the handful of separate but until now confusing little incidents started to add up, "when you disappeared a couple of weeks ago and missed that conference call with a soft-drink sponsor, was it so you could go to a funeral?" He'd come back extremely subdued and hadn't even managed a cheerful and encouraging word for Harry, who had been in a towering rage at losing the soft-drink sponsorship because the star of the show had missed the preliminary meeting. *Later* Redd had perked up and reminded Harry that it was a carrot-flavored soft drink that was remarkably terrible tasting and had impressively low sales, thus saving Bethy from having to explain to her brother that neither their show nor the soft-drink manufacturer had any money for advertising.

"I didn't speak or anything," Redd said. "I wore a sweatshirt and a baseball cap and sunglasses so no one would recognize me!" Which meant that he'd been remarkably lucky he hadn't been arrested for looking like the Unabomber. Bethy stared at Redd in horror. "I wasn't contacted by the family and I hadn't spoken to Elsie in years," Redd explained, "but there were a bunch of trees in the cemetery and I wanted to leave flowers for her after the ceremony."

"So, you hid in a tree."

"It wasn't my day in the limelight?" Redd offered. "I should have told you and Harry but—she died in a car accident and it was sudden, and I didn't know it had happened until you sent me that email of background info for the next three episodes."

Bethy wasn't sure which was more alarming—that Redd had learned of the funeral of an old friend through Bethy's background information, or that he'd just admitted he actually read those emails.

"You sent me a link to the Edgewater Archive because of that web exhibit on the Florida state parks," Redd explained. "Elsie's web exhibit on Florida shipwrecks was scrolling right next to it, and they had a memorial page up for her at the end of the exhibit. I didn't want to make everything more complicated for you and Harry, and Elsie was a really old friend—"

"Robin," Bethy said firmly, getting to her feet,

"come here and let me give you a hug? I'm not going to blame you for being upset about losing an old friend." She gave him a side-hug and patted him on the shoulder, because Redd was taller than Bethy and his hat got in the way.

"Although you might want to actually tell the Kingsolvers that you knew their aunt if we're going to keep running into them," she added. "Chris was pretty badly freaked out by the way you managed to disappear between the boat and the police station, and it's not as though—oh no."

"Um."

"Were you also trying to hide from Kevin McRae?"

"Maybe?"

"Redd!"

CHAPTER
SIX

THE HANDFUL OF PEOPLE WHO MET ON THE STONE benches outside the local college were a strange lot, and also a very groggy one. Carrie wasn't sure that her cousin's newest idea was a *good* idea, either. Searching Professor Griffin's office for clues was the sort of thing they ought to leave to the police, and Carrie half suspected that Chris only suggested it because he was at loose ends. Professor Griffin was in the wind, the treasure of the *San Telmo* was up in the air, and nobody was sure who to trust anymore. At least searching Professor Griffin's office gave Chris something to do besides wonder where, exactly, he had gone wrong.

Of course the person who had probably gone wrong was Carrie. If Professor Griffin hadn't found the *San Telmo* yet—and the lack of excited Professor Griffin arranging interviews with television studios suggested that he hadn't—then it must be because he had not found anything at the coordinates Carrie had so carefully and painstakingly researched. She'd even told him that they were a guesstimate, and not an exact location, so he should know not to give up if the ship wasn't just sitting there waiting!

Carrie had been up late the last two nights, wishing all her books on the location of the *San Telmo* weren't still in the clutches of Professor Griffin and going over what little she did have again and again, trying to come up with a reason the coordinates were wrong. It was almost a relief that Chris had shifted his focus to Professor Griffin with a vengeance, because it meant he wasn't asking Carrie to explain how she'd messed up because *she didn't know*.

Although she could've done without the new complication of Robin Redd being Robin Wyzowski—and thus the last member of Aunt Elsie's treasure-hunting club.

From the faintly bewildered way Dr. McRae was staring at Chris, it was clear that Dr. McRae couldn't quite understand what was going through Chris's mind at the moment or how he fit into all this either. Or maybe he was just not sure what he was doing breaking into an oceanography professor's office at eight o'clock on a weekday morning.

"We aren't breaking in," Chris said, shifting from foot to foot. "The building's open in the summer for the summer students."

"At eight thirty," Dr. McRae said patiently.

"We have to be sure nobody gets in before us?" Chris suggested. Dr. McRae tilted his head thoughtfully and actually conceded the point, and Carrie gave up on trying to make the world, or her friends, make sense. Instead, she took the coffee cup away from Maddison before Maddison—who was sitting

111

on the bench and had been gradually drifting back to sleep for the past ten minutes—finally gave in and conked out, which prevented her from spilling her drink everywhere.

"She's probably not going to get around to drinking that," Dr. McRae said, just as the groundskeeper for the college pulled into the parking lot, walked up the sidewalk, and gave them all a very unimpressed look. "So, if you like hot chocolate go ahead and have at it. Hi, Jim!" he added, as the groundskeeper opened the door with a jangle of his keys and continued to look unimpressed.

He paused in the now-open doorway, said, "Do not trample my flowers," to Dr. McRae and Chris, and headed for the basement.

"It was just the one time!" Chris protested.

"I dropped *one* book out the window," Dr. McRae grumbled, and gently gave his daughter's shoulder a shake.

"I didn't eat the tulips!" Maddison gasped, jolting awake. "Ow," she added, standing up and trying to ease a crick out of her neck. "Remind me why we're doing this again?"

"Frankly, I have no idea," Carrie said, sticking the coffee cup behind a pillar on the building's front porch, and they followed Chris and Dr. McRae inside.

✗ ✗ ✗

Professor Griffin's office was still familiar and homey, and that was the very worst part. Carrie knew that he had tried to leave her and her cousin in the ocean, but she'd been left to amuse herself in Professor Griffin's cheerfully book-cluttered office so often as a child that the room itself conjured up comforting impressions. Professor Griffin making his bust of Melville talk in funny voices, the taste of Jolly Ranchers—it was hard to shake the good memories. The professor almost always had some hard candy on hand, although anything so sensible as a candy dish escaped him and so they tended to be scattered around the bookshelves in seashell holders. In the process of flipping on a light Chris managed to knock one to the ground.

"Wow," Maddison said when they were blinking in the sudden brightness and Chris was picking up Jolly Ranchers. "This is not what I expected a homicidal oceanography professor's office to look like. And that's a lot of books."

"I'm glad to see he didn't lose that interest in Melville," Dr. McRae said faintly, reaching out one finger to poke the bust of Melville in the nose. "What, exactly, are we *looking* for?"

"Anything . . . suspicious?" Chris offered, and Carrie, Maddison, and Dr. McRae all turned as one to glare at him. But nobody had a better plan, so Maddison started systematically checking the bookshelves from one direction and Chris took the other and Carrie took it on herself to start going through desk drawers.

She found a lot of papers, most of them on oceanography topics she didn't have the time to figure out.

In fact, more than half of them were essays in the process of being graded, and she felt funny about reading them so she set them aside. There were also one or two flash drives in the top desk drawer, and a laptop computer in the second.

"Here, let me," Dr. McRae said, looking up from where he was checking the pockets of the two coats hanging on the peg by the door.

"It's password protected," Carrie told him, and then watched in amazement when Dr. McRae studied the screen for a thoughtful second and then got the password right the first time.

"His password's almost always 'Melville,'" Dr. McRae explained, squinting at the screen.

But there was nothing of any interest on the computer. In fact, there was nothing of any interest on the computer even to a student of Professor Griffin's, and it seemed that the professor had done nothing more sinister with the machine than check his e-mail. The flash drives were backups of old academic papers and lecture notes. And the books stuffed into bookcases all along the four walls of the office were just books, with no levers to secret passages or hidden compartments among them.

Chris and Maddison were going very slowly and checking for both anyway, although Carrie doubted there was going to be a secret passage in a building built in the seventies. Especially not when she knew from listening to other professors complain to Professor Griffin and Aunt Elsie that office space was rare and fiercely hoarded in a building that was too small for all the professors who had to cram offices into it. If there *had* been a secret passageway, three more people would have desks in it than could comfortably fit.

The professor's coat pockets turned up nothing more than a stick of gum and the keychain that had been lost for three years, and the trash can had been emptied so recently that the only thing in it was a single Kleenex. Carrie was just about to suggest that there was nothing in Professor Griffin's office that could tell them where the professor had gone or what his next move might be when the door to the office suddenly swung open, and Robin Redd started to walk through before he realized that the room was already full of people and froze.

Suddenly, Chris's determination to get to the office before it opened in the morning in order to enter before anyone else did was sensible, and not his paranoia talking.

Greeting someone first thing in the morning with the comment "You look exhausted" was generally considered rude, but Michelle hadn't survived as long as she had by being delicately polite. And Detective Hermann really did look exhausted, hugging his coffee cup like he was afraid it was going to run away before he could drink it. He'd poured it from the pot that had been sitting out all night and then dumped six packs of sugar into the cup, so it *was* actually possible that the coffee would make a break for it, or maybe make a break for an officer's weapon, but Detective Hermann was gripping it so tightly any escape would be short lived. Still, the detective had been about to head home last night when Michelle herself had dragged Forrest off to their hotel room, so why was he this exhausted?

"There was an attempted burglary five minutes after you left," Detective Hermann explained in answer to Michelle's unspoken question. "A very strange one, someone broke into Jeanette Tran's house and tried to make off with her local research. Jeanette Tran's the most enthusiastic of the local amateur genealogists," he explained.

"And they dumped this one on you because?" Michelle asked.

"Ah, no, I volunteered to look into it," Detective Hermann said. "Mrs. Tran was incensed because the person who broke in tried to make off with her research notes on Saint Erasmus Catholic Church."

"You've got to be kidding me," Michelle said. It had *not* escaped her notice that the priest at Saint

Erasmus had been turning away a variety of what he had called "people even odder than what I usually get," all of whom had been interested in the *San Telmo*, or the Kingsolver cousins, or both. And the dead body the kids had found in the church cistern, despite what the CIA had half hoped, had not been the body of Cesar Francisco but rather that of Ryan Moore. As a consequence, the FBI was investigating a cold case and the CIA was still wondering about the final end of a Cuban revolutionary. So, what was Griffin trying to hide from them now?

"Sadly, no," Detective Hermann said. "I wish I was kidding." He took a huge gulp of coffee, made a face at the taste, and hauled his briefcase up onto the table. "There wasn't much in Mrs. Tran's research that can't be duplicated, but I did manage to find one thing." He pulled a camera card out of the bag, and followed it with a printed-and-stapled sheaf of printer paper. Michelle took the paper with a frown and he shrugged. "Mrs. Tran likes working with paper much more than she does working on the computer. She had her granddaughter take these last summer when they were looking at regular church attendance versus the visitors. It's the church visitor log."

Michelle flipped through the pages and then stopped. "This was taken before the page in the visitors' log was ripped out," she said slowly, running a finger down the list of names from the early nineties. "And Ryan Moore—"

"Wrote his own name, and that of Willis Griffin, on the log the night he disappeared," Detective Hermann said.

✘ ✘ ✘

The evidence in Ryan Moore's own hand that he'd been in the church with Willis Griffin the night he was murdered was evidence that needed to be dealt with right away, and so even though she had her phone on vibrate in her bag, Michelle didn't actually catch the e-mail until she stopped to have a Danish and a cup of coffee at about eleven o'clock. Which was terrible for her blood sugar and her eating habits, but Forrest was dealing with Harvey the reluctant accomplice, and wasn't here to looked pained at her.

Michelle pulled out her phone, took a large bite of slightly stale apple Danish, and then almost choked when she realized that Lyndon actually had sent her something.

I'm not sure how much help this will be, he'd written in the body of the email, it was written specifically so that the person doing the confessing didn't get anyone else in trouble, and was sent to me after her death. But it might help you understand the man you're dealing with, if nothing else.

PS, I did print everything when I received it, but there was nothing on the letter itself and the envelope had over a hundred fingerprints on it—it was sent regular mail—and none of them raised any flags.

Attached to the email were a series of JPEGs. Coffee and Danish now forgotten, Michelle appropriated a computer from one of the officers going to lunch and opened the pictures. The first was an envelope, clearly good-quality stationery and with no return address. The second, third, and fourth were the three pages of a hand-written letter, written in elegant cursive, which Michelle enlarged to a readable size and then read.

Dear Gregory Lyndon,

You are an intelligent man, and so I shall not insult your intelligence by pretending you do not know why I am writing this. You came to me seven years ago, two years after a young man named Ryan Moore disappeared in Ridgeland Township. You asked me if I had any concerns, as a city councilwoman, about the officers from Fourtrees sent to Ridgeland to assist you; what you were really trying to learn was what I knew, and what I suspected, my son had done to his roommate. I'm afraid I sent you away rather harshly, and for that I am truly sorry. I respect good police work, and I hindered you in the process of seeking justice.

The truth is that you were right to be suspicious. The men I convinced our then–police chief to send to Ridgeland were fools, all of them. That most have washed out of the force I can only consider a blessing. I encouraged Hill to send them because I believed they would not even be capable of locating a suspect in the disappearance of Moore, and would waste time and resources until the case went cold. A sin, yes, but a minor one; Moore I believed to be willingly missing in the wake of a violent quarrel, and no good could come from my son's involvement in that incident becoming public knowledge. He was, and is, my only child, and he is a kind, generous, intelligent soul. His one flaw lies in an inability to let others beat him at anything and a tendency towards selfishness and obsessiveness, but these are faults possessed by many. That is not an excuse for my behavior, but it is an explanation for my behavior. I truly believed that he had said and done something unforgivable but not fatal, and that a missing-persons case was unnecessary and likely to cause my family undue embarrassment. That Officers Dall and Jameston so determinedly pursued Kevin Greenwood as a suspect was not my intention, and had he been arrested and charged I would have supplied legal defense out of my own pocket; likewise, I was prepared to use my connections at certain academic institutions to further his academic career had he been unable to continue his education as a result of the investigation. Greenwood proved more determined and capable than his detractors, however, and I truly believed that the entire incident was a regrettable but harmless abuse of my position.

However, seven years have passed since Moore went missing and he has not resurfaced, and I am now dying, and I find that I cannot rest easy *with the burden of this secret. I will not tell you what my son did to cause Ryan Moore to vanish, for to be quite honest, I do not know. But you of all people deserve to know that the investigation into the disappearance was hindered on purpose by shoddy police work, and that it was done to protect Willis Griffin.*

Sincerely yours,

E. G.

Beneath that was a postscript, added later and with shakier handwriting. It read:

Willis and Moore shared one interest that I can recall. They were both determined to locate the final resting place of a ship called the "San Telmo."

"I truly believed that he had said and done something unforgivable but not fatal," Michelle said to herself. "That's a parent for you. The kid's killed someone and she can't bring herself to confront it."

Reading between the lines of the letter, Michelle suspected that the writer, presumably Willis Griffin's mother—she would have to look up the woman's obituary to be sure—actually did suspect that Griffin had killed Moore, but couldn't bring herself to face that truth, let alone admit it in writing to another person. But Michelle saved the letter anyway, because, although it lacked almost anything that might help them convict Griffin directly, it tied Griffin to Ryan Moore and suggested that Griffin had something to do with Moore's disappearance.

CHAPTER SEVEN

ROBIN REDD MIGHT HAVE BEEN THE STAR OF A television show that was mediocre at best, Maddison thought, but he had a spine made out of steel in certain situations. Like this one.

"Fancy meeting you here," he said lightly, neither flinching nor turning to flee at the sight of the four of them. He took a step inside the office and removed his hat.

". . . yeah," Chris said suspiciously. "What are you here for?"

"Well," Redd said, spinning his hat on one finger. "The thing is, I happen to know this Professor

Griffin rather well from when we were schoolboys together—"

Maddison's dad huffed. Offended laughter at its finest.

"And I'm more than a little annoyed at him for dumping people overboard. He could at least have waited until International Talk Like A Pirate Day, when it would have been thematically appropriate."

Maddison felt one eyebrow rising under its own steam.

"And then," Redd said, "I found out from talking to the park ranger at Grey Cove that Griffin's boat, or, I suppose, the boat that Willis Griffin was in the habit of taking out on the water, was found in pieces on the shores of the island this morning—"

"Wait, *what*?" Carrie asked. "Professor Griffin crashed his boat? But the water was calm last night!" Suddenly her eyes widened and the blood drained out of her face. "My library books!"

"*Moby*!" Chris added, equally horrified.

Redd shook his head. "I said it was found in

pieces, I didn't say it crashed. And if *Moby* is that submersible the girl was wrangling out of a car in the front parking lot then *Moby* is quite fine."

"Okay . . . " Chris said faintly.

"Robin, *what are you doing here?*" Maddison's dad asked, frustration leaking into his words.

"Looking for Willis's next move!" Redd exclaimed, startled into giving a short and sweet answer. He didn't seem comfortable being in the same room as Maddison's dad. Come to think of it, Maddison's dad didn't seem at all comfortable being in the same room as Redd. Maddison thought about Chris's paranoia and how often he was sort of or mostly right and began to hope fervently that this wasn't going to be a repeat of the Professor Griffin difficulty. But Mr. Lyndon had seemed to think Redd had no masterminding inclinations, and her dad had laughed in delight when he'd realized that Redd was the person who had fished Chris and Carrie out of the ocean.

Maddison *had* yelled at him a bit for not

bothering to mention to her that Robin Redd was the same person as Robin Wyzowski, to which her dad had mournfully replied that he didn't think it mattered all that much. At the time she'd been too confused and angry to do much more than glare at him, but now Maddison had to wonder why he didn't think it mattered all that much. Had they had a falling out? Was Redd really the mastermind behind all this? How did either Chris or Redd expect to find a clue to Professor Griffin's next move in a perfectly ordinary office?

She asked that last question, and Chris just sighed. Red looked suddenly very guilty.

"I did try to look for clues to his next move in his house," he admitted. "But I'm afraid that didn't net me anything, and the police have the house under surveillance so I almost got arrested on the way out."

Maddison's dad buried his face in his hands.

"But this is his office," Redd said, moseying over to the desk and shifting a stack of partially graded essays aside. "It's a much better place to hide the things you don't want anyone to know about, since it's so much easier to claim that somebody else snuck in and the dead porcupine was in no way at all yours, but it's also not the first place people turn when they want to look for your secret hiding places." He looked *inside* a tiny plastic pencil sharpener. "And it's a much more public space so if the police decide to search here they won't have an excuse to get angry at me." He sat down on the desk itself. "Most people will insist on assuming that you've got a safe or a loose floorboard in your bedroom . . . "

Maddison snuck a glance at Chris, who looked a little uncomfortable and was probably now wondering how safe his hiding place for his aunt's letter was.

"And look for that before they consider the fake bottom of a desk drawer at your place of employment."

Redd leaned back on the desk—and leaned right into the bust of Melville, knocking it over. It rolled in a crooked circle on the desk, and had just come to a halt when Redd grabbed for it and his fingers slipped on Melville's shiny ceramic head.

With a *thunk* and a crash, the bust of Melville fell off Professor Griffin's desk and hit the floor, breaking into three pieces as it did. There was a ringing moment of silence, and then Maddison's dad broke the silence by smacking himself in the forehead.

"Robin," he said, pained.

"Don't worry, Chris has broken, like, three of them," Carrie said. "One time the professor bought a new one to replace the one Chris had just knocked off the shelf and Chris didn't realize it was on the desk chair and he sat on it and it cracked right down the middle."

"I'm a little less worried about replacing Willis's desk decorations and a little more worried about what the police are going to think when they eventually decide to serve a search warrant on this office and they find Robin's fingerprints all over a recently broken statue," her dad said in a strained voice.

"Oh, chill," Redd said, getting off the desk, this

time without knocking anything over. He pulled a blue-and-yellow handkerchief out of his pocket and shook it out with an entirely absentminded dramatic flourish, and then bent to pick up the biggest piece of Melville. "I'll wipe the pieces down and dump them in a trash can and nobody will be the wiser . . . huh."

"What's 'huh'?" Chris asked. Maddison's dad was *glaring* at Redd with way more venom than even the goofiest of television hosts ought to be bringing out. What issues did the two of them have?

"See here?" Redd asked, tilting the biggest piece of Melville into the light. "This impression in . . . it looks like hot glue, almost?"

"That looks like a key," Chris said. "A boat key."

"The perfect impression of a key," Redd said thoughtfully. "This was stuck together with putty, by the way," he added, scraping a fingernail along one of the "broken" edges. "Pity, that makes it hard for us to tell when he removed the key."

Maddison took the piece of Melville from Redd

when he offered it to her, and squinted. "I think you can actually make out the insignia on the key," she said. "If we took this to the police they might be able to find out what kind of boat it came from." She passed the piece of Melville over Chris's shoulder to Carrie, who looked closely at it, and then froze.

"And that will tell us what kind of boat Professor Griffin is out there sailing around on," Chris suggested. He didn't look terribly happy. "It just figures he had a *secret boat* that nobody knew about." Behind him Carrie set the piece of Melville down on the carpeted office floor hurriedly and yanked her phone out of her pocket. Then she stared at it, wide eyed.

"And he let me think I was cursed to break statues all these years, when really he had his busts of Melville pre-broken and then put back together so he could get at the key at a moment's notice!" Chris continued, warming to his subject. But before he got into a passionate lecture on Professor Griffin's failings as a statue curator, Carrie interrupted her cousin by bursting into hysterical giggles.

"Carrie?" Chris asked.

"Oh—I just—it's just—I can't *believe*—" She was crying and gasping for breath. Maddison's dad yanked the desk chair out and offered it to her.

"Sit down before you hyperventilate," he said firmly. "What did you just realize?"

Carrie had to take a few sobbing, hiccupping breaths before she got her lungs under control, but then she looked down at her phone and said, "I couldn't figure out why he didn't find the *San Telmo*."

"Professor Griffin?" Redd asked gently. Maddison's dad glanced up at him sharply. Maddison really needed to figure out what the problem was between the two of them.

"Yeah," Carrie said, "Professor Griffin. Who I handed the coordinates to, because I thought I could trust him." She swallowed. "But if he found the *San Telmo*, then he wouldn't have left the boat washed up on the shore, and he wouldn't have tried to break into Aunt Elsie's house, and he wouldn't even still be trying to hide what he did to Ryan Moore. Because I don't think he's going to care about *anything* after he finds that ship. He wouldn't be trying to break into his own house, either," she added, "except that wasn't even Professor Griffin . . . " Carrie trailed off significantly.

"Yeah, that was me," Redd said. Under everyone's exasperated looks he blushed sheepishly. "I just wanted to figure out where he went after he ditched *The Vanishing Triangle*," he reiterated. "But Griffin doesn't keep anything incriminating in his house, so he must keep everything here, or have a secret lair or something."

"Or something," Maddison's dad muttered.

"Carrie, you were saying?" Maddison said before her dad could get into a fight with Redd or do something equally ridiculous.

"But I couldn't figure out what must be wrong with the coordinates I gave Professor Griffin until just now, when I was looking at the impression the key made," Carrie said. "That's when I realized: I wrote down the latitude and longitude *backwards,* because I worked out the points backwards. I reversed the numbers," Carrie admitted, shifting uncomfortably under four intense gazes.

"I got nervous and I wasn't paying attention and I wrote them down—" She grabbed a marker and a clean pad of paper from the desk. "I put the coordinates down as 12.3 45 67; 8.9 10 11 but I reversed them," she said, scribbling out an example. "He was looking in the wrong place because the numbers I gave him were wrong, not because the clues Aunt Elsie left us were wrong. It's like looking at this imprint of a key—the impressions aren't exactly what you see when you find the real key, they're the *reverse.* Professor Griffin has the right coordinates; he just doesn't know that I wrote them down the wrong way around!"

"What if he turned the paper upside down?" Chris asked.

"Wouldn't work," said Maddison, who had just figured out what Carrie had been trying to explain. "It's not like nineteen becoming sixty-one when you turn the paper over, it's like one, two, three, four, five being written down as five, four, three, two, one."

"It's *that* simple a mix-up that's keeping Professor Griffin from finding the *San Telmo*?" Chris said.

"Be very thankful for the small things," Redd said.

CHAPTER EIGHT

WILLIS GRIFFIN WAS COMING UNGLUED, although he didn't seem to realize it and Brad wasn't going to point it out. In fact, Brad was beginning to suspect that Harvey, wimp that he was, had done the smart thing in bolting the moment they had set foot on land. Getting arrested would be preferable to following Griffin around while he muttered distractedly to himself and tried to break into various houses, although Brad was beginning to realize, with a cold, creeping feeling of dread, that Professor Griffin was most likely going to kill himself before letting himself get arrested. And that was if the guy actually ended up in a shootout. For a college professor, Griffin was scarily good at avoiding the cops.

He'd ditched the college's boat by setting the autopilot and steering the boat directly into a beach, muttering under his breath about nosey park rangers the whole time. But not before going crazy on the deck with the emergency hatchet—he'd managed to cut whole pieces of the fiberglass hull off with that thing before he ran out of energy and relocated himself, Brad, Harvey, the Kingsolver girl's backpack, and the robot-thing into a life raft. They'd watched *The Vanishing Triangle* crush itself into the sand from offshore, and then paddled to dry land themselves because Griffin insisted on putting his precious submersible somewhere out of danger. For a horrible moment Brad had been sure that the man was going to drag them all the way back to the freaking college to put the submersible back, but then he'd just hidden it by the bathrooms. Harvey had staggered off into the woods at about that point, looking green, and then just not come back, the useless coward.

"Well, that's disappointing," Griffin had said to Brad, hands on his hips. "I do hope you didn't care for him overly much, he might end up in a good deal of trouble."

Then the crazy college professor had set off on a cross-country hike that eventually led them to a nearly deserted trailer park on the less-inhabited side of the island, where he kept a barn with a car "that isn't registered in my name" inside. "I had to let Cliff use it to, err, deal with someone recently," Griffin had explained. "But the police *should* be done looking for the car since they caught the driver."

It had occurred to Brad then, as it hadn't when he and Harvey took the job, that Harvey's bud Cliff wasn't the type to commit suicide. And it was awfully convenient for this professor guy, Cliff dying after getting arrested for the hit-and-run. But Brad hadn't had time to get nervous about being with Griffin—probably a good thing, and maybe the reason he wasn't yet the subject of a mysterious "accident"—because the professor needed a lookout driver while he "checked some sources."

Brad then spent half an hour parked in a random driveway watching a plastic bag that was caught on a tree flutter pathetically in the wind. Griffin took yet another hike through the woods; he came back panting for breath, empty handed, and in a nasty mood.

"They're being rather more perceptive than I realized," he said.

"Who?" Brad had dared to ask, and Griffin had scowled and told him that the Kingsolvers were somehow fine and dandy and on dry land again.

"I can't imagine who they managed to get help from," Griffin said darkly, "unless that blasted McRae decided not to run away after all. But I sowed all the right seeds for doubt, so why they would trust him . . . " He had trailed off, looking wistful, for some strange reason.

"Anyway," he'd snapped suddenly, "it hardly matters. If the kiddies are poking around their aunt's things then that means they're back at square one, so we'll have to"—they'd both jumped a mile when the phone rang. And then things went from terrible and confusing to even more terrible and confusing, because the call was from Griffin's actor friend Aaron, who had quickly abandoned his career as an FBI agent and taken the first bus out of town, with the real FBI hot on his heels. Because Aaron had a hot tip: the FBI agents were not, it appeared, planning on leaving.

"What do you mean, they identified the body?" Griffin had demanded, and then he had gone completely white.

"I see," he had said, and then hung up and stared into the middle distance for a full fifteen minutes. Brad counted, out of horrified fascination. He'd never actually met someone who stared into the middle distance before, he'd thought that was just a thing people did in movies.

"There is only one place it could still exist," Griffin had finally said. He hadn't, of course, bothered to explain what "it" was. Instead, they'd gone back into town, waited until dusk, and tried to break into the house of some old woman who did genealogy research. Emphasis on the *tried*, because she had three dogs that all started barking the instant they heard Brad working on the window, and then the old lady herself came tearing out the front door carrying an honest-to-goodness frying pan, and they'd had to book it without getting whatever Griffin wanted. That had made Griffin's mood, if possible, even blacker than it had been before, and Brad had almost been glad when his next move had been to break into the college—Brad hadn't done this much burglary since he was eleven—and start smashing statues. But at least they actually managed to break into the professor's office without being seen, and Griffin found the boat key he was looking for.

So now they were on Willis Griffin's boat, the one he stored in an abandoned marina with a bunch of excavating equipment and a lot of scribbled-over maps, safe in open water but without a clue what to do next. Griffin was pacing back and forth on the deck; he'd let Brad steer but had demanded that Brad take them in circles. Brad was seriously considering throwing himself overboard. He'd signed up to make a quick bundle of cash; he hadn't signed up to deal with some wacky psychopath who had an obsession with sunken treasure and people who had Kingsolver for a last name.

"Huh," Griffin said suddenly, flinging—yep, that had been his cell phone—into the water. He had a yellow sticky note in his hand. "The key to the coordinates," he said grimly to the sticky note, "is still in the Kingsolvers. If I can't solve it, they can't . . . but they haven't given up yet, have they?" He turned to Brad, who gulped. "*Have they?*"

"No?" Brad offered.

"Precisely!" Professor Griffin said, his expression suddenly sunny again. "We need to head back to Archer's Grove."

This, Brad thought but didn't dare voice aloud, *is the worst job I've ever taken.*

✗ ✗ ✗

Detective Hermann sat down at the computer and, with a growing frown, read the letter Michelle had pulled up. When he got to the end of the page he just sat there for a moment, staring at the screen, before putting his head in his hands, and sighing. Then he wordlessly handed a slip of pink paper—normally used for taking messages—to Michelle.

"The head librarian at the downtown branch library just reported that a bag of their books was left on the library steps before they opened for the day," she said.

"Tandy reported it because some of the books weren't library books and four of them had the same name in permanent marker on the spines. She just thought the whole situation was strange and it was ringing enough alarm bells that she felt it best to call it in. The report got bumped to *me*—"

"Because the name on the books is Kingsolver," Michelle said. Detective Hermann nodded. Michelle sat down in the desk chair across from Detective Hermann, the better to put her own head in her hands and sigh. "So, we have one wrecked ship," she said, "one old disappearance-turned-murder; one new hit-and-run that was really a murder; one suicide under mysterious circumstances; one possible case of police misconduct; one confession that tells us nothing; one missing oceanography professor; one archivist with a dark cloud over his past; three attempted break-ins; two Kingsolver cousins—"

"And a partridge in a pear tree?"

"Please don't tempt fate," Michelle said. "I would not be surprised if one actually turned up."

CHAPTER NINE

MADDISON WAITED UNTIL THEY WERE HALFWAY down the hallway before she made her move. And she made sure that her move was *decisive*.

"Uh, Mads?" her dad asked. Chris and Carrie looked impressively unsurprised, as though they'd been expecting her to do something drastic all morning and were just glad it wasn't happening on the roof.

"Sorry," Maddison said, planting her feet and grabbing one handle of the double doors that led to the stairs—and the only way out of the building—with each hand. "But I peeked as we came in and these offices are all deserted, and this is a hall-way with no other exit unless you want to go out the emergency fire escape doors. And *that* sets off an alarm that calls the fire department. So, I'm not letting you out until you and Redd explain why you can't handle being in the same room with each other."

"I can handle being in the same room with him!" Maddison's dad protested. Redd, in contrast, looked like he was seriously thinking about taking his chances with the fire department. Chris gave him a measuring look and then sat down directly in front of the door leading to the fire escape. Carrie looked around and then just dropped to the floor where she was.

"Despite what Chris thinks—" Maddison started to say, before she was interrupted.

"Hey!" Chris protested. "I'm naturally paranoid and someone I really trusted just threw me into the ocean, give me a break!"

"We are," everyone else in the room said.

"And you jumped," Carrie said primly. "*I'm* the one who was thrown."

"A-ny-way," Maddison said, "despite what Chris thinks, there's no reason not to trust Robin Redd and every reason to think he's on our side."

"Thank you." Redd was, however, regarding Maddison warily.

"So, I kind of need to know why my own dad can't handle being in the room with him, and why *he's* so nervous around my dad."

Redd and her dad exchanged glances. Then something hardened in both their expressions and they both took a half step farther apart rather than offering an explanation. Maddison fought down the urge to pull her hair out or shake both her dad and the television star. For one thing, she liked her hair. And for another, she was much too small to pick up her dad, let alone Redd.

"Can I ask a question?" Carrie interrupted. "Because I think it's related and I only just realized it." Not waiting for a response, she went on. "Of the five of us here," she said, "only one knows what happened between Professor Griffin and Aunt Elsie and Robin Wyzowski when Ryan Moore went missing, right? Because Maddison said that Dr. McRae never knew why everyone stopped talking to him. So, Redd." She turned to the television star. "What happened?"

Redd stared at Carrie. Then he turned to Maddison's dad. "You don't—oh," he said. Then he whirled around and punched the wall, hissing a stream of swears under his breath. They were either really obscure or in a foreign language or both, because Maddison only recognized two or three. "That vicious little—*fluff*," he finished, *fluff* quite obviously not being the word he had initially wanted to use. "Kevin, Willis told me and Elsie that Ryan went out with you that night to look at some old ruins in the middle of a swamp somewhere."

Maddison's dad opened and closed his mouth and finally said, "And you *believed* him?"

"Well, what were we supposed to think? You and

Ryan had had a screaming match the day before and you were having a spat with Elsie! And then— Ryan talked my ear off about some new direction he wanted to take the research on the *San Telmo*, something about a Spanish mission church and a parish register? He told me he was going to go look at an old mission church that night. He didn't actually tell me who he was going to go with, but when Griffin said he saw you two leaving—"

"*He said what?*"

"You didn't know," Redd said, eyes wide. "Elsie stopped talking to *all* of us, Griffin went around acting all concerned and explaining away why you went somewhere with Ryan—and doing it really badly, dear blessed *ratings* that makes a horrible sort of sense—and I couldn't get you alone to talk to you, and—and you didn't even do what Griffin claimed you did."

"You couldn't get me alone because I was getting dragged down to the police station every other day and asked a lot of leading questions," Maddison's dad said faintly. He'd been leaning against the wall with his arms crossed and his ankles crossed and every line of his body announcing that he did not want to have this conversation, but as Redd had gone on Maddison's dad's arms had dropped to his sides and now he slid down the wall till he was sitting on the floor. "And I *didn't tell them about the San Telmo.*"

He dug both hands into his hair as though he would very much like to start pulling it out in frustration (and horror) himself.

"But I *did*," Redd said. "I told two different police officers about what Ryan had said, and I explained to both of them that Ryan was into treasure hunting! They didn't think to ask you?"

"I get the impression that nobody wanted to add treasure hunting into the mix," Maddison said quietly. "And as long as only one person mentioned it, and they were already a source of . . . unusual theories . . . "

"You suggested aliens, didn't you," Maddison's

dad said. It was not a question. "You panicked, and when Robin Wyzowski panics he starts babbling whatever comes into his head and you'd just been reading about abductions."

"So, they just discounted everything I said," Redd said faintly. "That would explain, well, a lot." He laughed. "It's even a good thing, because I was the only person who thought there might have been jealousy involved."

"Jealousy?" Maddison asked. The look on Redd's face was ugly, but it wasn't directed at any of *them*. Maddison's dad, meanwhile, looked very slightly stunned.

"Kevin and Elsie had just had a fight about dating," Redd explained. He sighed and sat down on the floor across from Maddison's dad, but noticeably outside striking distance. "I don't actually think they considered it a fight about dating," he added, when Maddison's dad moved to interrupt. "By the time they stormed off in different directions—don't argue, you did, it was almost choreographed it was so neatly done—the fight was about grad school interviews. *But*," he continued, "Elsie had at one time had a bit of a crush on Kevin, and Kevin had at one time had a crush on Elsie, and Elsie was thinking of asking Ryan Moore to the dance that was coming up. Except she felt guilty that she didn't have a crush on you anymore," Redd added. Maddison's dad was blushing and looking stricken at the same time. "You felt I-don't-even-know-what about the fact that you hadn't realized you had a crush on Elsie until Willis said something to you about it, and poor Ryan didn't have a clue what was going on. I think mainly because he had that French class when you and Elsie had your big fight, so by the time he found us you were both off sulking somewhere and Willis and I were trying to decide who got to calm down which friend."

"I was trying to get her to see that Willis was planning to ask her to that dance," Maddison's dad said miserably. "He'd told me offhandedly the day before, and I didn't think it was going to work out for him at all—she only ever saw him as a friend—but I didn't really want to find out what Willis would do if she turned him down flat out of surprise."

"Elsie would hardly have been mean to him," Redd said.

"Willis was weird about Elsie," Maddison's dad said grimly.

"So, who actually went to the dance with whom?" Carrie asked. They were, by this point, all sitting in an accidental circle facing one another with Redd and Maddison's dad at equal points on opposite sides. At Carrie's words everyone turned to give her a bewildered look.

"We know there was an argument," Carrie said stubbornly, "but not how it all shook out. So, who went to the dance with whom? It might tell us who *made up* with whom."

"Nobody went to the dance," Redd explained. "Ryan disappeared and none of us felt like partying; Kevin was under a huge cloud of suspicion; Elsie was really broken up by everything, and I was halfway down the road to hysterical. Willis and Elsie spent a lot of time in the library studying together—*fluff*."

He was getting good at subbing in innocent words for swear words at a second's notice; there hadn't even been a stammer. Also the implications of what Redd had just described were terrible.

"Aunt Elsie was never anything other than best friends with Professor Griffin," Carrie said carefully. "We did sometimes wonder why she never ever considered dating anyone . . ."

"We did?" Chris asked. "I just assumed she had a tragic love story in her past." Carrie scowled at him, but since they were on opposite sides of the hallway she couldn't quite reach him to punch him.

"You don't think Willis would've done something to his competition, do you?" Maddison's dad asked Redd.

"The timing is a bit suspicious."

"But Ryan was also the most into treasure hunting, aside from Willis. We've already got plenty of evidence that Willis is obsessed with finding that ship. Do we really even need to bring romance into it?"

"But if we bring romance into it, then we have a possible explanation for why he tried so hard to frame you, and left me alone," Redd said. Maddison spared a moment to wonder if he knew that when he got really into something his dramatic speech habits disappeared. "Secondary motive, but still essential to explaining why he went after you."

"And it could explain why he went so far as to get rid of Ryan—Mads, why are you smiling?"

"Oh," Maddison said happily, "I'm just so glad you guys are talking again!"

✗ ✗ ✗

Professor Griffin had never before had difficulty sleeping. He had also never before spent quite so much time running around taking care of difficult tasks under the necessary cover of darkness, but he was hardly a stranger to the need for stealing in after dark and quietly removing a little something that might become difficult later on. But difficulty sleeping? That had never happened to Professor Willis Griffin before.

Oh, he had run-of-the-mill nightmares, and strange dreams about palm trees, and vision after vision of the *San Telmo*—beautiful, elusive ship that she was, but nightmares were a sign of a guilty conscience, and his was clear.

Willis Griffin pulled the blanket farther over his head, on the cot in the cabin of his fallback boat, and reminded himself sternly that he needed his rest. He had to appear tired but in control when he approached the Kingsolvers and fed them a convincing lie about what had happened on *The Vanishing Triangle,* and to do that he needed to *construct* a convincing lie about what had happened on *The Vanishing Triangle,* and to do *that* he needed his rest.

But in order to rest he had to close his eyes and

fall asleep, and the long-gone face of Ryan Moore kept swimming to his mind's eye when he did.

It had not been planned, what had happened to Ryan, and as far as Willis was concerned, it really had been an accident. A random combination of events and circumstances that led the two boys— they'd been nothing but boys, then—to a Catholic church that had open doors and empty pews, and a lock on the basement door that was easy to pick, and a dead-end cistern that had suddenly become an opportunity.

They'd been peering over the edge through the flimsy plywood covering and tossing pebbles into the depths when Ryan had said, "You know, this might not be a complete loss?"

"Yes, the ghost of this cistern is going to pop out and tell us where the *San Telmo* lies buried if we only throw in the right combination of pebbles," Willis had replied, and Ryan had laughed, and told him that while that would be convenient, he actually meant that they were looking in the wrong place by looking in the church itself.

"Think about it," he'd said. "If I were a parish register, where would I hide? Not in some dusty unused cistern! I'll bet you anything that if we go ask the parish priest he can point us to the old church documents and we can get something out of those."

"You're right," Willis had said, and then *it* had happened. Ryan had been balanced on one of the sturdier of the wooden planks covering the cistern— he had an excellent sense of balance—but as he'd laughed and moved to join Willis on solid ground in order to go ask the priest about the parish register, he had slipped. And then he had fallen.

When Willis had rushed to the edge of the cistern Ryan had been clinging to the plank for dear life, eyes wide but not all that scared. Willis was there, he was capable—Ryan had nothing to be afraid of. The thought still stung a little. Betrayal always hurt in the quiet moments.

"Gimme a hand, would you?" Ryan had asked,

breathless. "And hurry, Willis"—he had been inter-rupted by a terrible groan of wood—"this beam isn't as sturdy as it looks!" In fact, there was a weak spot just a hair from the point where the plank met solid ground, where the wood was almost splintered in half all the way through. Willis grabbed that end, with nothing more sinister than an idea of pulling the plank closer and the weak spot away from the edge, and then something rose in him. It wasn't quite jealousy, it wasn't quite anger, it wasn't quite greed and it was not at all hate—it was some mix of a dozen different emotions, all of them screaming at him that he had one perfect chance, and that he couldn't afford to waste it. And Willis Griffin had never been one for wasting his own chances.

It took one single blow from his fist to snap the already weakened wood clean in half. It broke with a dull cracking sound, and then Ryan seemed to hang in midair for a second, and then he fell. He didn't even have time to get mad about it; Willis met his eyes for a half second before Ryan hit the ground with a wet thump and his eyes were wide and shocked and hurt.

And then his eyes were open and unseeing, because—because Willis hadn't seen a dead body before, but there was no way you got up when your neck was twisted the way Ryan's was. Willis dragged a piece of particle board across the cistern opening until it naturally blocked any view of the body, and then he rubbed a handful of mud across the freshly splintered board until it looked like an old break, and then he rubbed out their footprints as he backed his way out of the cistern room.

He did it all in a sort of calm haze, and it wasn't until he was in the car, driving back to the college— because it would *not* be a good idea to start asking questions about the *San Telmo* that very night, because he had no idea who Ryan might have told of his thoughts—that the enormity of what he'd done had set in.

A lesser man might have quailed; Willis Griffin rose to the occasion. They had taken Ryan's car to the church, which was a great convenience, as it allowed Willis to sink the car in the swamp before he returned to the dorm. Then he played the part of a confused and worried friend when Ryan failed to appear at breakfast. He was not the one last seen to have quarreled with Ryan, so suspicion did not fall on him and it was easy enough to direct it toward other people. When the police eventually got involved, he let his mother suspect that he knew more than he was able to tell, and she obligingly did her best to keep the investigation from going anywhere. By the time he took a TA position at a college in Maine, the disappearance of Ryan Moore was old news, and his tenuous ties to an old police case went unremarked on. Losing Elsie and Robin to grief and confusion was a terrible blow, and although he never did get back in touch with Robin, who buried his grief in a history degree and then an insane jump to reality television, he could have cried when he caught up with Elsie again after years apart.

She never quite slid back into their comfortable

friendship, though. Elsie alone, out of all of Willis's friends, could have guessed what he had done, and although he was still sure that she hadn't, he was never again as unguarded around her as he had once been.

He'd thought, sometimes, of bringing her back into the search for the *San Telmo*. Elsie Kingsolver was quick and clever and good at puzzles, and as the years dragged on and Willis's private search for the ship went in nothing but circles, he yearned to tell her. For that was the greatest frustration of all—once Willis had been certain that the search for Ryan had died down, he had gone in search of the clue for which Ryan had given his life. And he had found nothing! The legendary parish register was missing! The existing manuscripts said *nothing* useful about the parish register! The church had no full-time historian! It had been one of the worst disappointments of Willis Griffin's life, and what was worse, he hadn't been able to get help for it, because every time he thought of talking to Elsie about the treasure he would catch her looking at him, as though she *knew* . . . no. It was better not to risk it.

He had gone more than a little mad when he realized Elsie herself had *stumbled* onto the location of the *San Telmo*. He'd been in her office looking to borrow a paper clip and the notes had been out on her desk—under another piece of paper and a few books but still, out on her desk, like a taunt.

Willis had been forced to act, and act fast, and he still didn't know just how far Elsie had come in her scheming before he'd caught on, or how much she suspected he knew, and he missed her *terribly*.

And now, for the first time in years, for the first time *ever,* he was dreaming every night of that terrible moment when he had watched Ryan Moore fall.

CHAPTER TEN

FORREST HOLLAND STOOD IN A LITTLE CEMETERY in the town of Fourtrees over a grave that was covered in moss and ivy, listening to his phone ring out. "Emily Griffin, beloved wife and mother," he said when Michelle finally picked up. "No, it wasn't hard to find at all, and the dates on her headstone would bear out what Lyndon told you. This is a dead end." He scuffed his foot through the overgrown grass. "But for what it's worth, I think she was telling the truth. Yeah, I'll be back as soon as I can."

He hung up, and then stepped back to fetch the plastic bag he'd brought with him. Michelle had asked him to speak to the Fourtrees police department about the officers loaned for the duration of the Ryan Moore case, and to see what evidence he could find that might support the not-really-a-confession sent to Lyndon. The first objective hadn't gone anywhere, mainly because, as Michelle had glumly suspected, nobody at the department now had been around when the Ryan Moore case had happened. Forrest agreed with Michelle's assessment of the deaths of three of the officers involved with the case as "highly suspicious" and in fact was surprised that Gregory Lyndon had escaped from the mess relatively unscathed, but then, Lyndon cut an imposing figure and he had been police chief at the time of the incident, and it was perfectly believable that nobody had dared to attack him, or risk drawing even more attention to themselves by getting another jurisdiction involved.

He'd had only slightly better luck with the anonymous letter. That it was from the mother of Willis Griffin was obvious, and Griffin's mother had been on the city council and friends with the police chief at the time Ryan Moore disappeared. Confirming her birth and death dates, and that she had in fact died of cancer, had been possible through the Fourtrees library's extensive newspaper collection, and he'd managed one lucky break in the form of an elderly postal worker who was eager to talk Forrest's ear off and had actually remembered the "fuss and kerfuffle" that occurred when a letter from the good lady went through the system a week after the will was read.

Meaning, miraculously enough, that the letter had actually been posted after the woman's possessions had been distributed and her last requests carried out. It wasn't that hard to counterfeit a letter from beyond the grave, since handwriting could be faked and arrangements made with unscrupulous third parties to post mail from all over, but the timing fit and the confession had a distinct ring of truth to it. Forrest had located the grave with no small amount of respect, and genuine relief at having a decent offering of flowers.

Forrest had stopped at a florist shop on his way out of Archer's Grove and picked up a simple bouquet of lilies. It was a technique he used all the time. A strange young man poking around town asking questions about the deceased or poking around the cemetery looking curious was going to get angry townsfolk in his face. That same young man with a bouquet of lilies asking about the deceased and poking around a cemetery reading gravestone inscriptions was looked on with a lot of sympathy. People imagined he was a distant family member and fell over themselves trying to be helpful. The only strange thing had been getting the flowers, because when Forrest had walked into the shop and asked for a bouquet of lilies, the girl behind the counter had automatically asked if he wanted asters with that. Puzzled, Forrest had asked her what on earth an aster was—he was somewhat familiar with various types of cactus because he had a sister who grew them professionally, but otherwise he paid no attention to plants unless it was useful for a case—and the girl had hauled an enormous bushel of pretty purple daisy-like flowers out from behind the counter.

"We usually only get a few in, but there's been a really weird fad for them this summer," she had explained. "So we had to start buying them in bulk, except not enough people come in to buy them to get rid of the excess we get when we buy them in bulk." She grimaced. "And they aren't the catchiest of flowers." They weren't. They were pretty, understated little things. But they looked like they'd go quite well with the lilies, so Forrest had agreeably added them to his order, and now he had a bouquet of white lilies and purple asters. It was an odd combination but the white and purple were pretty together, and there were worse things than mismatched flowers.

"Michelle is still mad nobody's caught Willis or found a confession that might stick," Forrest said politely to the departed spirit of Emily Griffin.

"But you did a decent thing, admitting the truth to Gregory Lyndon, and nobody ever thanked you for it, so I will." He nestled the flowers against the headstone. "Thank you for being brave enough to admit what had happened, even if it wasn't until the end."

Not that it was any help in finding Willis Griffin or convicting him of the trail of murders he was leaving behind, but at least they now knew why the case had been handled so badly the first time around.

✗ ✗ ✗

Bethy Bradlaw was not looking for a treasure map. In fact, she was hoping to put the *San Telmo* and Redd's craziness behind her for the afternoon, and was instead interested only in a particular legend about the fountain of youth and a manatee-obsessed merchant.

Over the course of a week and a half she had dealt with two different attempted murders and one fake federal agent, and had lost about a quarter of the footage her brother had planned to get due to disruption, disaster, and the threat of all their cameras being confiscated by the police. Then Redd was having even more trouble than he usually did staying focused on one legend and had vetoed or accidentally sabotaged the *San Telmo* segment, the bit about ghost manatees, and three other sound bites, once by sitting on the bug they were trying to film. Bethy was running out of ideas and material that could be accessed and then shot by a perpetually understaffed and underprepared film crew while the star of the show had the ghosts of his past come out to haunt him. She'd been listlessly skimming through a book of local legends and seriously considering sending Redd on a search for the Swamp Ape when she'd caught a single-sentence mention of a fountain of youth, and since that sounded appropriately Floridian and decidedly unlike anything Redd had spent his college years hunting, she had immediately gone looking for more information about it.

Unfortunately, there was next to nothing about

the local fountain of youth online, at the local library, or at the local bookstore, and the librarian had agreeably explained to Bethy that except for a single manuscript describing the supposed location of the fountain, no documentation existed anywhere.

"But the Edgewater Archive has a really nice reading room and they're open to the public Monday through Thursday," the librarian had added, "so if you want to go read the manuscript for yourself, you can."

Which was why Bethy was tucked away in the corner of the archive's reading room, two boxes on the cart beside her. This archive allowed the use of cameras, as long as you didn't use the flash, and Bethy had taken a half-dozen notes on the fountain of youth, gotten an excellent picture of the manuscript that she could force Redd to examine before they started shooting. She then had decided that while she was there she might as well do some of the more detailed research work she needed for the segment on manatees.

Edgewater held the papers of Richard E. Emanate, a local merchant locally famous for his theory that manatees were the mermaids of legend, which in turn were the lost souls of women who drowned at sea. He had devoted his life to finding a way to return the poor things to human form, and had been Archer's Grove's earliest proponent of manatee protection, even if for a completely insane reason. *There might possibly be something in the water around Archer's Grove*, Bethy thought. And not just overflow from the fountain of youth.

What Bethy wanted now were a few interesting quotes from the merchant protector of manatees, who had by all accounts been a charismatic and inspiring leader. Unfortunately, his papers had been given only the briefest organization and description before they had been made available to the public, and so Bethy was forced to shuffle through all three boxes of material on Richard E. Emanate looking for his writings. He'd produced a lot of letters in his life, had left behind stacks of accounting slips, save-the-manatees raffle tickets, and even two led-gers. Going through the boxes was fascinating but it also took forever. And it was almost impossible to tell what some of the papers were about until you read them! That was why, when Bethy opened a folder that she hoped would hold a picture of the merchant and three vellum pages fell out, she hardly noticed that they weren't related to the man at all. But then she thought to skim the pages for a useable quote and suddenly she was more than a little alarmed.

Now, Redd had tried as hard as he could to avoid telling Bethy or the rest of the crew anything about the *San Telmo*, citing, at various points, the fact that the ship was cursed, the fact that the ship was *not* cursed, and a firm belief that if Bethy had to deal with one more police officer asking her questions she was going to run screaming into the night. Frankly, Bethy had no idea if *Santa Maria Estrella de la Mar* had anything to do with the *San Telmo*. But she had a healthy respect for Murphy's Law, and bitter experience had taught her that if it was possible for something to go wrong it would, so when she realized that the three vellum pages were not by or about Richard E. Emanate, and were instead church records written in Spanish, she promptly stuffed them back into the folder, *behind* the picture of Emanate that was supposed to be in the folder, and flipped the folder shut. Then she did some very fast thinking.

The sensible thing to do would be to take the obviously misplaced papers to the archivist on staff. But the head archivist at Edgewater had died under suspicious circumstances and her immediate replacement had recently been placed in protective custody. If she took these pages to the college student manning the front desk there was a decent chance of getting that girl either killed or arrested. So, feeling the entire time like the worst sort of criminal in existence, Bethy took the papers out of the folder, waited until the girl at the desk was fetching a box for a visitor, and then closed the papers into her laptop. Then she put her laptop back into its case, packed away the boxes she had been using, and when there was again someone at the desk to sign her out, gathered her things as casually as she could, and left.

She felt the entire time as though she had an enormous target painted on her back, but she must have been sneakier than she thought because nobody looked twice at her. Bethy still didn't relax until she was sitting in her car with the doors locked, and then she called the only person she could think of who might know what to do.

"Redd, I can't believe I'm saying this, but I need a little advice . . . "

✗ ✗ ✗

"The problem with the *San Telmo*," Gregory Lyndon explained, "is that nobody wants to admit it's a factor in the investigation."

Michelle realized that she'd opened a can of worms. She had only intended to call in order to thank him for sending her the letter from Willis

Griffin's mother, but then he'd asked if the treasure ship was factoring into her investigation. This led her to ask when it had come up in the investigation of the original disappearance. She was now realizing that Lyndon had been quietly chipping away at this case on his own time for years, and had opinions on it.

The *San Telmo* was obviously part of the problem, in that Griffin had an almost unhealthy obsession with finding it, but that was to be expected with people who were experiencing a slow but total descent into madness, and she said as much.

"And that's true," Lyndon said. "But Griffin was obsessed with finding that ship *before* he started murdering people. McRae never thought to mention it, but the thread tying him to Moore to Griffin to Wyzowski and even to Elsie Kingsolver was the *San Telmo*. I didn't find out until just this week that the Kingsolver cousins are fulfilling a last request for their aunt in trying to find the *San Telmo* themselves." Which neither kid had told Detective

Hermann, Michelle realized irritably. "That ship is the focal point of the whole investigation," Lyndon explained. "Or I should say, the way people seem to go crazy when they get serious about finding that ship is the focal point of the whole investigation. I wouldn't be surprised if Griffin is still in the area, still trying his hardest to find the *San Telmo* even when he knows you've got the whole island on high alert looking for him."

"And I'm inclined to agree with you," Michelle said. "But that still leaves me with the question of where he is. If he was the one trying to break into Elsie Kingsolver's old house we couldn't catch him, he hasn't been back to his house, and we have his car and the remnants of the boat he used. He can't just vanish into thin air!"

The door opened. Michelle had been pacing back and forth along the desks in the bull pen, occasionally reflexively tidying paperwork on the desks as she passed, and keeping an eye on the door. Forrest was due back from his trip to Fourtrees at any moment, so as soon as she heard the door she glanced up. Then she almost dropped the phone in bewildered surprise.

"Agent Grey," Dr. McRae said awkwardly, edging through the doorway like he expected her to snarl at him. He had a clear plastic garbage bag with a collection of smashed pottery in it, and his daughter was stuck to his side as if with glue. She looked like she desperately needed a nap and was worried that her dad was going to cut and run. Chris and Carrie Kingsolver were right behind the McRaes, Carrie looking almost as exhausted as Maddison. And to top off all the ridiculousness, Robin Redd was bringing up the rear of their odd little group, his dramatic hat in his hands and his expression strangely determined.

"Hi," Michelle said dubiously.

"What's Kevin done *now?*" Gregory Lyndon asked on the other end of the phone, and Michelle rattled off an "I'll call you back later" and hung up on him, the better to have her hands free to deal with whatever she needed to do when every person of interest in this investigation save for Griffin himself walked in the door at the same time.

"So, I stopped by the college to see if I could grab a book I lent Griffin back before the whole building got cordoned off with caution tape," McRae said, which was one of the most transparent lies Michelle had ever seen, "and while I was looking I knocked a statue off his desk, and long story short did you know Griffin may have had a boat nobody knew about? Because if so we've found the impression of the key for it."

Remember when you thought parrot smuggling was going to be the strangest thing you ever saw? Michelle asked herself, as Robin Redd's phone went off and he tried to answer it without making any noise.

"I'm back," Forrest said, choosing that moment to come in through the back door with six evidence boxes in his arms. "And I got some decent background info from the folks in Fourtrees, although I've got to ask, did you know there was a fad for asters at all the florist shops in Florida? It's the weirdest . . . thing . . ." He'd finally set his boxes down in a pile on the floor, and looked up.

"Asters are turning into a fad?" Chris Kingsolver asked. He looked like he desperately wanted to laugh but was afraid it would be impolite.

"I think I've missed something," Forrest said.